Hannah's Story: Vampire Love Never Dies

GIULIETTA MARIA SPUDICH

iUniverse, Inc.
New York   Bloomington

Hannah's Story: Vampire Love Never Dies

iUniverse books may be ordered through booksellers or by contacting:

iUniverse
1663 Liberty Drive
Bloomington, IN 47403
www.iuniverse.com
1-800-Authors (1-800-288-4677)

Because of the dynamic nature of the Internet, any Web addresses or links contained in this book may have changed since publication and may no longer be valid. The views expressed in this work are solely those of the author and do not necessarily reflect the views of the publisher, and the publisher hereby disclaims any responsibility for them.

ISBN: 978-1-4401-3502-6 (sc)
ISBN: 978-1-4401-3501-9 (ebook)

Printed in the United States of America

iUniverse rev. date: 04/16/2009

To my family

Chapter 1 – Arrival

It began like this. Hannah Tramont got off the plane in London and took the escalator down to the airport subway stop. She bought a ticket from a gray and blue machine, her first purchase using British pounds. She picked through the coins for five minutes, trying to identify their values. The coins felt heavy in her hands—especially the two-pound coin, a gigantic disc. She was finally rewarded with a thin paper ticket. Once she got onto the crammed subway, it was only about a twenty-minute ride to the station named Earl's Court. She felt greasy from the long flight, and, after the hot subway ride, she felt even sweatier. She was relieved to reach the street, and at first the thin rain felt clean and cool on her skin. She soon started to feel cold, however, so she began to walk quickly. Unfortunately, this caused her suitcase to bang against her knee as she walked. In only a few minutes, she was soaked. Her normally smooth, straight, well-combed hair was wet and long strands of it stuck to her face. She was relieved when the door to the Emmett Hotel emerged, sandwiched between two tall, gray houses. She felt even happier to see a little café just across the street, where they offered coffee and croissants.

She could use a coffee. Hannah hesitated before entering the hotel. She hated to have to speak to the people at the reception desk knowing how wet she looked. She tried to smooth her hair back, as she knew it must be plastered to her face. She wrung out some of the water and pulled her hair back into a ponytail. She opened the heavy door to the hotel.

The man behind the tiny wooden reception desk gave her a cheerful smile as she entered.

"Wet enough for you, love?" he asked amiably.

Hannah smiled in return but could not meet his eyes. She must look like she had just dragged herself off the street, she worried.

"Booking for Hannah Tramont, please? My Aunt Laura booked it," she explained. The man produced a key after checking his files and nodding to himself. He asked to see her passport, which she displayed, and he pointed to a narrow staircase.

"One floor up," he explained. "We don't have a lift."

Hannah began to climb the stairs, her suitcase banging against her knee again. She thought about the word "lift." It sounded so airy—much more fun than a weighty "elevator."

She sighed with relief when she reached the little blue door of Room 18. Her knee felt bruised from the case, and she had a small headache from the long flight. When she tried to force the key into the lock, however, it just would not fit. Jiggling it for a few minutes, Hannah finally got the key completely into the lock. But it wouldn't turn.

After a few more minutes of wrestling with the key, her hand now red where she had pressed against it, she made her way down the stairs once again, dragging her bag behind her.

The man at the reception desk looked up, startled.

"Is the room not all right, love?" he asked.

"No, no … I mean, it's fine. Actually, I don't know. I can't get in. The key won't work," Hannah explained, her head starting to pound.

"Ah, there's a trick. Let me show you."

The man was larger than he had looked when he was hidden by the wooden reception desk. He heaved himself up and moved toward Hannah. He took the key from her and then grabbed her bag with one hand, easily maneuvering it up the stairs. Hannah said a grateful thank-you.

"I'm George, if you should need anything else," he said to her as he wrestled with the key.

There was a horrible wrenching noise, and then the door swung open. Hannah stepped inside. The room felt warm, and, though it was tiny, it looked cozy. A double bed waited invitingly for her, and when she peered into the connecting bathroom, she couldn't decide between sleep or a very hot bath. George left her then, saying breakfast was served from six to nine. Hannah remembered the little café she had seen next to the hotel. A coffee sounded so good, but she first wanted to dry off or maybe sleep. She was so confused. She closed the little door.

The door didn't lock, and she had lost the will to wrestle with the little metal key again. Besides, she was afraid she might accidentally lock herself in. She took off her soaked tennis shoes and placed them by the tiny radiator. Then she peeled off her socks and placed them on top of the heater. She sank down on the edge of her bed, thinking about what to do.

The wind howled outside, and rain pelted her window. She stared at her suitcase, willing it to open so she could change into warm, dry clothes. Her fleece pajamas would be perfect, she thought. Hannah was just too tired, however, to reach over and actually open the case. Instead, she lay down on the bed.

She turned and looked at the unlocked door. Was that dangerous? Then she giggled. Hannah found it ironic, since, for the first time in a long time, she felt safe.

She had left everything to make a new start, here in rainy England. She smiled, despite her pounding head. She could sleep without worrying about anyone finding her in the night. She had walked through the dark rain without fear. She closed her eyes and drifted off to sleep. When she woke up, her socks were warm and dry, so she slipped them back on her feet and curled up in the bed with her suitcase propped against the door. She slept for twelve hours. The rain never stopped.

She awoke around noon the next day, and when she stretched, her back made a cracking noise. She gasped when she looked in the mirror. Her hair was so greasy, it looked two shades darker. She took a hot shower, and discovered a huge bruise on her knee. The shower loosened her joints, and she could stretch without cracking now. She had slept way past the hotel breakfast, so she went to the café next door and ordered a coffee and two croissants.

And for the first time in a long time, as she licked the sugar off her fingers and watched people stamp their tall boots through puddles, Hannah felt happy. No one but her family, whom she trusted, knew where she was.

Tomorrow she would move into her new college in Cambridge and unpack in her new room. She hoped the door would lock.

It began like this. But really, it had begun much earlier.

Chapter 2 – Cambridge

Two days after her arrival in London, on October 3, 2008, Hannah Tramont walked out of her biology class. Lecture, she reminded herself. They call it "lecture" here, not "class." The classroom had been spartan and not very warm. Now, on the cobblestone street, Hannah shivered in the wet air. Her dark, straight hair was unruly in the humidity and uncharacteristically wild around her smooth, oval face. She looked up at the sky. The rain had stopped, but the sky was not exactly what Hannah would call clear. It looked like San Francisco on a foggy day. Well, she thought, the clouds were at least higher than the San Francisco fog. She could almost imagine blue behind that mother-of-pearl ceiling of clouds above her.

Perfect weather for … no. Hannah bit her lip. None of that mattered now. She didn't even want to think of the monsters she had left behind. She shivered. Just the thought of Bret and his gang made her feel colder than she already had. Hannah suddenly heard the sound of clicking boots approaching from behind her. They clicked faster and faster on the cobblestones and almost seemed intent on catching up with her.

"It's impossible," Hannah said to herself. "I don't

know anyone here." She bit her lip once again.

The tap on her shoulder made her jump. When she turned, she was relieved to recognize the girl who had sat next to her in biology class, the one who had lent her a pen. Hannah took in her lively brown curls; wide, friendly eyes; and round, smiling face. She felt relaxed at once.

"Hi. Hannah, right? We didn't get a chance to talk in class. Are you on your way to maths?" the girl asked.

"Yeah … how'd you know?" Hannah asked, silently thinking, Maths? Why plural?

"We biology master's students tend to have the same classes. Cell biology, statistics, evolution. Am I right?"

"Yes. Those are my classes. Except in the U.S. we just call it math. Not maths." Hannah smiled.

"In the States, you mean?" the girl countered her smile with a larger one. "Yeah, I hear everything's a bit off over there."

Hannah laughed.

"So that's where you're from, then? Where in the States?"

"Oh, you know," Hannah replied, evading the question with a hand wave. "It's a big country." She shifted the pile of books; it was getting heavy. "I've never been to England before." Hannah tried to change the subject.

"Well, I'm Lily. Consider me your personal tour guide." Lily stopped walking and peered up and down at Hannah's thin rain jacket, jeans, and sneakers. "Well," she commented from inside her faux-fur–collared coat and her warm-looking, furry boots. "You may want to get a heavier coat."

Hannah sighed and looked up again at the dark, gray sky.

Lily suddenly smiled and waved in the direction of a group of boys talking to each other.

"Ah. Here we have the first stop of the tour. That …" she said, pointing to a tall, lanky boy with extremely white teeth, "… is Matthew, the most gorgeous boy on campus."

"Oh, so that's a boy. They look different in the U.S."

Lily laughed. "You're all right," she said and punched Hannah's arm playfully. They both watched Matthew as he grinned and clapped a hand jovially on one of his friends' shoulders.

Lily leaned in and whispered, "They've been playing polo all summer. That's why they are so tan and so toned."

Hannah guffawed.

"So … what do you think?" Lily asked, her eyes gleaming.

"Oh, are you interested in him?" Hannah asked.

"Not for me, for you!" Lily exclaimed. "I've got a bloke." At this, Lily raised her hand to show off a ruby-colored ring with shiny diamondlike … diamondlike …

"Oh my gosh, are those real?" Hannah gaped.

"Yup," Lily smacked her lips. "He's rich. Don't get me wrong, I would love him anyway." They both exchanged a smile. "And so? I hear Matthew likes Americans. He finds them exotic."

"Oh, no." Hannah suddenly found her pile of books slipping. She had noticed in class that Lily had only a binder with her, with photocopies of the chapters they were working on that day. Hannah made a mental note to lose the stack of books as soon as possible.

"No, no boys," she managed to say. "I'm here to study."

"What, no boys?" Lily took in Hannah's dark, soft hair; smooth, olive skin; and green eyes. "With that face, I reckoned you would be a regular man magnet."

"Look, I'm just not interested. I need ti … time. To get over my ex … B … Bret." The pile of books slipped dangerously as the blond Matthew turned his gaze toward Hannah and smiled.

"Oh, look at that!" Lily grabbed Hannah's arm. "Let me introduce you!"

"No, I'm serious!" Hannah wrenched her arm away from Lily's grasp with more force than had she intended to. The books tumbled to the wet ground.

"All right, okay," Lily said in an alarmed tone. "I was only trying to introduce you. It isn't easy being the new girl, I know."

"No, I mean, yes, I mean, it's just that …" Hannah averted her eyes as she scraped the books together. This day was turning out to be more intense than Hannah had wanted. "It's just that I b … broke up with someone."

"Oh, this Bret, right. Broken heart?" Lily asked, suddenly understanding, her brown eyes wide. She reached out and patted Hannah's shoulder.

"Yeah," Hannah answered. "Broken everything."

Once Hannah had all her books in a neat stack, Lily linked her arm through Hannah's. "Right, no men. But can there still be fun?"

For the second time in as long as she remembered, Hannah smiled freely. She felt the creases around her eyes lift. "Oh!" Hannah suddenly remembered and took a pink and gold pen out of her pocket. "This is yours. Thanks again."

"Don't be daft, you'll need it for mathsssss," Lily emphasized the *s*.

Hannah laughed. "I would say, don't be silly!"

"Silly!" Lily guffawed. "That's just ridiculous, what a stupid word, silly!"

They walked off to class, laughing at each other's expressions all the way. Hannah tried not to notice the tan, joking boys watching them go.

Chapter 3 – On Her Knees

Two weeks had passed, and Hannah still had to stop in front of King's College and gaze at the old, stone college building every time she came near it. The spires and stained-glass windows made it look like a castle or a palace. She had already taken fifty or so pictures of the college from every possible angle, by day, by night, and in early morning, and had sent them on-line to her mother and aunt (who had asked her to take some pictures of other things in Cambridge ... and maybe some people—friends, even?) She couldn't help it if she found it so fascinating and beautiful. "1500s," she muttered to herself. She could not really grasp how old that was. She remembered a house in Illinois that had been built in the 1880s—she had seen it with her parents. She had thought that was so old and had wanted to touch the old, peeling wallpaper. (She hadn't been allowed to, though). But of course it wasn't really all that old.

No, she hadn't ever seen anything so old ...

Suddenly an image snapped into her mind. She could smell the smoke of the Trellis bar, one of Bret's favorite hangouts. A hard, cold, metal object had been pressed into her palm. His eyes—emerald, so piercingly green even in this dim light—swam into her mind like smoke.

She had looked into her palm. Light reflected off a pearl encased in an oval ring of gold. The gold was fashioned into a leaf pattern, and it looked old and hard, as though it had seen centuries pass. Yet it shone with its original beauty.

She heard his breathy voice, low and softly accented. "It was in my family for generations. My great-great-grandmother's. I have carried it all these years. Now it is yours."

Light shimmered off the pearl. "Oh …" she had gasped. "It's beautiful." He had gracefully plucked the necklace out of her small palm and raised his arms to her neck. He had fastened the pearl there. Her heart had beat, beat so strongly. She thought of never taking it off. But of course it was taken back. Everything had been taken back.

Hannah's knees gave out, and she found herself kneeling in front of the great college.

"I know it's grand," a jovial voice said in her ear, "but I haven't seen that reaction before." A strong hand gently took her arm and lifted her back to her feet. She turned to meet a pair of light blue eyes. They sparkled as if they contained small pieces of glass or bright gems. The tall, lanky boy was smiling at her. It was Matthew. Hannah hadn't noticed just how tall he was—at least a foot taller than she was. His face was tanned and freckled from the sun. As she stared, still partly in the world of that dark bar, his light eyes shifted to a deeper color and looked concerned.

"You all right?" he asked.

She blinked and smoothed her skirt, trying to bring

herself back to Cambridge, back to this moment. But the music, the soft music of that bar, still lingered in her mind.

"I … I think it's just the jet lag," Hannah reasoned.

"Ah!" A spark shot through his eyes. "American!"

Hannah remembered what Lily had said about Matthew liking Americans, and she blushed.

"That explains it. You probably have never seen anything older than a couple centuries!"

Hannah had to laugh. "Maybe … try just one century!"

Matthew studied her face for a moment. "Well, you know the best cure for jet lag?" Hannah raised her eyebrows. "King's coffee." Matthew motioned to the towering college building, and Hannah gasped. Iron locks covered the huge wooden door.

"We can drink coffee in there?" she asked, amazed.

"Of course! Some students live in there." Hannah's knees wobbled, and Matthew steered her carefully inside a smaller, less frightening door, carved into the larger one. They entered the college grounds. To Hannah it was like passing through a castle wall.

"You must be in one of the newer colleges. Have you got that pass yet—the blue pass?" Hannah nodded dumbly as they entered a huge court with perfectly cut green grass. Just to the left was an entrance to the college bar.

"Well," Matthew continued, "that will get you into any college, any time. And they all have a bar." He looked into her green eyes and winked. She giggled.

As they headed into the bar, Hannah took in the modern decor. It seemed at odds with the sixteenth-century building. The red plastic cushions of the sofas and the perfectly square tables resembled something more American than English. Hannah suddenly realized she was drawing the intense and scornful gaze of a very tall, dark-haired girl dressed entirely in scarlet. The girl scowled.

"Um ... should I know her?" Hannah asked, pointing at the girl.

Matthew glanced over, and his face grew tired. "Oh, that's Emily. She's my ex."

"Oh. She looks nice," Hannah said with irony.

"Oh, believe me, she's even nicer than she looks. I still have scratch marks. Mathematician ... and so calculating," Matthew said morosely and then caught himself. He studied Hannah's face. "Apologies, that's not a ... a gentlemanly thing to say, is it?"

Wanting to alleviate the mood, Hannah replied, "Oh it's okay, I almost have bite marks from my last ..." To her relief, Matthew laughed, but she herself could not believe that she had brought Him up so flippantly. "He doesn't belong here," Hannah reminded herself. She was not to think about him. The music from the Trellis bar in San Francisco came back into her mind, but she focused instead on the Madonna song playing in the King's bar.

"So, one King's coffee, brewed the same way since 1500?" Matthew asked jovially. Hannah believed him for a second but then realized he was joking. She hit him lightly on the arm with her glove. Matthew patted her back, chuckling, and ordered two cappuccinos. Hannah noticed the scarlet-clad Emily staring a hole into her and shivered.

Matthew turned to her and said, "Maybe you should

have some whiskey in that! Get rid of that chill. It's only October, love. The winter is still coming … "

"Yeah," Hannah admitted. "I'm not prepared for winter. I need a heavier coat," she said, gesturing to her rain jacket, which was far too light.

Matthew looked at her jacket and grinned. "Either a new coat, or a warm arm to wrap around you on those cold wintry nights … "

Hannah blushed. "Are you always this forward?" she asked, embarrassed.

"Um … not really." Matthew's forehead wrinkled in thought. "Okay, yes. Mostly. When I see something I like." He smiled, his eyes reminding her of shining gems again, and Hannah blushed even more deeply.

"Are you really very cold?" Matthew asked as Hannah wrapped her fingers around the hot mug of cappuccino the girl behind the bar gave her. "Because if you're cold, you can have this," Matthew said, gesturing to his sweater.

"No, thanks. I'll warm up with the coffee. Wait, what are you doing?" Hannah looked horrified as Matthew started to take off his sweater. "I mean, thanks, but no, I don't need your sweater … just the coffee." Hannah's words stumbled out of her mouth.

Matthew grinned but smoothed the sweater back down over his chest. "It's quite fun shocking you. I don't even mean to do it."

Hannah eyed the sweater as Matthew's eyes danced across her face, as if he was assessing her. The sweater did look warm. She would have taken it if he had been her boyfriend. She blushed to think about it. She would have to get a heavier coat soon, and possibly heavier sweaters.

She was staring at his face now and realized how blue his eyes actually were. Bluer than the stripes on his sweater, she thought. Their eyes met.

Hannah tried to ignore Emily's fuming glare from across the bar. "I think I just feel a little cold because where I'm from—San Francisco—it's four in the morning!" Hannah explained. Then she bit her lip. Not only had she brought her past boyfriend into the conversation, she had mentioned where she lived. She had wanted to keep her origins vague for as long as she could.

"So, a California girl!" Matthew said, smiling. "Well, you have been here what … at least two weeks now? You're on England time now, love." Matthew touched her arm and gestured toward a table. As they walked to the table, Matthew whistled, "Wish they all could be California girls," by the Beach Boys, and Hannah noticed Emily listening and then rolling her eyes. So much for subtlety, thought Hannah.

"So, gotta bloke back home?" Matthew asked as soon as they sat down.

"You're so direct!" Hannah exclaimed, laughing. "I thought you English people were supposed to be subtle!"

"Oh yeah, we are. We drink tea as well, and wear really ugly sweaters and call them jumpers." He raised the cappuccino to his lips and toasted Hannah. Then he thought for a moment. "Do you hate the jumper? Is it actually ugly, and I'm under some cultural illusion that it's not?" He looked horrified, and Hannah laughed. "Is that why you rejected it?"

"No," Hannah soothed him. "I'm just not that cold," she lied. "It's a lovely sweater. It's even a nice jumper. And it matches your eyes."

Again, Hannah bit her lip. She really hadn't meant to mention anything about it matching his eyes.

"So, seriously, before I lose my heart to you: are you dating someone back home?"

Hannah was struck by his sudden serious expression. She sighed. "Okay, no, I have no ... what you said, 'bloke.'"

Matthew smiled, showing all his brightly white teeth. "Except for biting man."

Hannah winced.

"Oh, sorry. Was it an ugly breakup?" Matthew asked.

Hannah couldn't help it. Her eyes misted over. "Sorry," she mumbled into her coffee. She took in one shaking breath. "It's just that ... I left him behind. But it wasn't that long ago."

Matthew looked at her with concern in his eyes. "Sorry ... no pressure ... you don't have to talk about him."

She nodded and gulped her cappuccino.

Matthew winked at her. "Just as long as you're single."

At this, Hannah laughed, and a little bit of foam blew over to Matthew's hand, breaking up the sad moment. She felt a glow in her cheeks that had nothing to do with the cappuccino and everything to do with the funny, engaging man across from her.

"So, what are you studying?" Matthew asked, changing the subject.

"Biology. I wanted to focus on biochemistry, but the research topics looked more inter—what?" Hannah broke off. Matthew's tan had suddenly disappeared, and his face was slightly pale.

"Oh, I didn't realize you were a brain! I took you for a musician. Well, I probably can't keep up with you, then!"

"What is that supposed to mean?" Hannah asked, confused.

"Well, I'm just a polo player, really. Though I am studying sports therapy, too. Mainly to apply to myself," Matthew joked, though his smile faltered.

"Well, I've never seen a polo game. It sounds interesting. Besides, you're friends with Lily, right? The girl with long, curly hair? She's in the same program as me."

"True, true," Matthew nodded. "I just … wow… biochemistry … find that intimidating."

"You study anatomy, right?" Hannah asked, and Matthew nodded. "It's the same thing! Only my classes are focused on more science, less coordination."

Matthew seemed to relax more, the flush in his cheeks coming back.

"And anyway, I guess I should worry more, since you're around tan, fit women all the time." Hannah bit her lip. "No men!" she said silently to herself. Matthew, however, caught her meaning and lit up.

"So, you are interested? I knew it!" he beamed.

"No, I mean … it's just …"

"Jet lag?" Matthew asked.

Hannah covered her face with her hands and then peered out at him through her fingers. They stared at each other for a moment, Matthew looking victorious.

"So, tell me about this polo," she said, once she felt

her face was less red.

For the rest of their coffee conversation, he told her polo-playing stories from the summer, and she looked suitably awed when he showed her the scar on his ankle where a horse had kicked him a few years back.

"Just nicked me. I was lucky, really."

Hannah laughed. In some ways, he seemed like an eager boy, ready to share adventures and laughter. She wondered what he had seen in the tall, perfectly dressed Emily. She didn't look like much fun, but then again, Hannah had to admit, she was beautiful, with that dark, glossy hair, scarlet, tight-fitting outfit, and high boots. Hannah shook her head. It didn't matter. She wasn't looking for a boyfriend. She would just be friends with Matthew. She leaned in closer as he showed her another scar, this one on his elbow.

Too soon, it was time for Hannah's study session. She had to admit that, against her will, she was letting down her defenses, having fun. As she and Matthew agreed to see each other for coffee another day, Hannah thought it might be true, she might really be starting over.

Chapter 4 – What Was Left

The next two weeks passed quickly. Hannah was busy with classes, and the various coffees with Matthew and Lily kept her mind occupied with her new life in Cambridge. She had decorated her little college room with pictures of her parents and Aunt Laura. There was a table by her double bed and also a chest of drawers, on top of which she placed pictures and candles. By college rules, she wasn't allowed to light the candles, but they smelled and looked so nice that Hannah bought them anyway. Resigned to the cold winter weather, she spent an afternoon shopping for a warm coat. Part of her actually looked forward to all the cozy studying in her new room. She had to admit, holing up in her room or the library was easier when it was cold and dark outside.

Lily threw Hannah a surprise birthday dinner on the 29 of October at the White Otter, a pub near their colleges. Hannah found it adorable. It was a small, dark place with lots of old wooden tables of different sizes all thrown together. Paintings and sketches of otters adorned the walls. The pub overlooked a street where Hannah watched students passing by, either pulling their coats tight around them or peering longingly into the warm pub.

Hannah had thought she would feel lonely on her birthday, but having dinner with the happy, joking Lily and four other students in the master's program took her mind off friends and family in San Francisco. Matthew had sent his apologies through Lily—he had an away match that weekend, so he could not join them. Hannah felt slightly disappointed that he couldn't come, and that surprised her. But then she thought about Bret and how horribly that relationship had ended, and how frightened she was now as a result. No, it's better this way, Hannah thought to herself. She should focus on friends only.

That night she checked her e-mail from her college room, lying on her bed. There was no other place to sit in her room. It was either, sit on the plastic chairs in the communal kitchen, or hang out on her bed. As Hannah checked her email, part of her hoped she would find something from Bret, though he had never e-mailed before. Would he really have forgotten her birthday? The year before, he had brought her to a candlelight dinner he had arranged on a boat, on the San Francisco Bay. They had eaten dinner (well, *she* had eaten dinner) as they floated on the dark water, watching the lights of the city. But this year, there was no note, no contact. She felt a mix of disappointment and relief. She told herself this was better; it just meant that Bret and his gang were really in her past. She read the e-cards from her aunt, her mother, and her friend Cindy. No mention from her mom of any dark-haired boys trying to find her … only birthday wishes.

It's better this way, Hannah reminded herself. A clean break from Bret. Anyway, it's safer.

She wrote back to her mom and her aunt, saying she'd had a great birthday dinner, and attached a picture of Lily and the others at the pub. She promised to tell them all about it in their first conversation on the phone; they had arranged for Hannah to call the next day. Hannah really had had a nice time at the pub and wanted to tell her mother all about it. She knew, however, that her mother would ask her to come home for the Christmas holidays when she called. Hannah just couldn't decide. On the one hand, if she stayed indoors during the evenings, she would probably be safe enough in San Francisco. Bret and Tressie were not interested in finding her, and Tobias and Jel, the dangerous ones, could not enter her house. But then again, she did not miss those sleepless nights, worrying whether one of the vampires … there, she had said it … would attack her. She had slept through the nights easily here in England, far away from Bret's gang. The dark circles under her eyes had finally receded into her normal skin color, making her look and feel healthier.

Fluffing up her pillow and letting her head sink into it, she decided to concentrate on the nice birthday dinner instead of worrying about the holidays. She replayed Lily's ringing laugh; it was such a contagious, full laugh, and Lily loved to use it. Hannah smiled. Then she found herself wondering where Matthew was. Was he asleep, too? Then she wondered where Bret was with Tressie. "No," she muttered into the pillow. She tried not to think about him as she fell asleep.

The next afternoon, she called home. Her mother commented on the lightness in her voice.

"You sound happy, dear. And those pictures are amazing," her mother gushed. "Is it really always gray there, though? I haven't seen one blue sky in the pictures."

"Well," Hannah replied. "They claim it's a particularly bad stretch of gray days, but I'm not sure I believe it!"

"Your friends look nice—the ones who took you out for your birthday."

"Oh yeah, Lily, the one with dark, curly hair—she decided to invite me and some of our classmates to a pub for my birthday. It was fun. They surprised me!"

"So, are you coming home for Christmas? Have you decided?" her mother asked. Hannah could hear her straining to keep the eagerness out of her voice. "No pressure. I know you just got started over there. "

Hannah sighed. She considered it once again in her mind. She had meant to stay away at least a year. But Lily and Matthew had told her how the whole town was devoid of students during Christmas break. Still, she was sure she could amuse herself some way, even if she was alone in Cambridge for all of break. She could always go to London; it would be fun to explore, even on her own. But her mother would be so disappointed if she missed coming home. And Hannah missed things, too. The sun. Seeing the blue water of the San Francisco Bay. Eating clam chowder in a bread bowl.

Besides, it had been months since the breakup. Bret and the others had probably even moved away. Anyway, even if they had stayed in San Francisco, there would be no reason for them to look for her. Not anymore.

Maybe, Hannah thought, repressing a chill when she thought of Them … maybe if she just went out with her mom and dad in the day, claiming exhaustion at night so she could stay home, she would be safe enough …

Hannah said decisively, "Okay, I'm coming. Can Aunt Laura get the tickets?"

Hannah heard nothing, then a whooping noise, and some clapping. She smiled and could almost see her mother dancing around the kitchen, clapping. Hannah guessed that her mother would be in her nightgown and robe, since it was morning in California. She was probably drinking a cup of coffee. Hannah felt happy thinking that soon, in just a month, she would see her mom in person. But then a cold feeling stole across her heart, tightening it—a feeling she remembered well but had not felt for weeks; she had been so absorbed in the warmth and friendliness she had found in Cambridge. She said good-bye to her now ecstatic mother and put down the phone. The cold feeling was still in her heart, so she went to the communal kitchen to make some hot chocolate. She decided to stay in her room and study for the evening.

Just three hours later, she received an e-mail from her mom, saying the tickets were booked: Hannah would go home for Christmas and New Year's. Hannah did not know whether to be nervous or happy about the trip back. She didn't want to put herself in danger again, but perhaps the danger was gone. Well, Hannah sighed, she had already said "yes" to her mom. The tickets were purchased. She would just have to hope nothing would happen in San Francisco. She would be careful.

It was only nine, but the sound of gentle rain was soothing, and she felt sleepy. Once Hannah crawled into her bed, she felt so warm under the covers that she immediately drifted off to sleep …

… and he was there again. There, so real, his emerald eyes boring into her, making her legs shake. The color of the stormy sea, she thought, that kind of green. He moved closer to her. They were in the billiards room adjacent to the bar. Her head swam and the dark room started to spin. She was about to fall. She reached out and steadied herself by holding onto his shoulders—so strong, she thought. Like marble. She could smell his shampoo, his cologne. Bret smelled smoky, pine-scented, and dark. He bent and kissed her neck, and her pulse raced. He backed away, then ran his hands through his hair, pulling it. "Hannah," his beautiful voice sounded tortured. "I don't know what to do. I don't …" They were alone in the shadowed room, since most of the customers had already gone home or were hanging out by the bar itself.

She couldn't move. Her legs felt like iron rods shoved into the floor; there was no way to back away. The only way she could go was forward, forward, into him. She wanted him. Her blood wanted him. She took a step toward him, and he raced up to meet her. His grasp felt stronger than before. He held her, and now she couldn't move for a different reason—his grasp was so strong. But she didn't want to move.

"One of us," he whispered, hot against her neck. "One of us," and he licked her. Her pulse flew to her neck, to his lips, and then agony crashed through her. She suddenly saw lights, then saw her hair and her face through his eyes. She tasted her own blood.

Hannah woke up covered in sweat; even her hair was wet. The rain had intensified, and the wind echoed in her heart like the chaos in her mind. She touched the scar on her neck. So faint, just visible, but it was always there.

It could have been worse, she reminded herself. If Jel hadn't walked in and pulled him off her, thrown him against the wall, she might have drunk. Drunk to save her life. Once Bret had drained her of her blood, she could either die or drink the blood in Bret's veins in order to survive as a vampire. Then she would have been just like them. A monster.

But she had ended up in the hospital emergency room with a lack of blood she could not explain, except to say she had given blood twice that week. Though there was no mark on her arm and two sharp, deep cuts on her neck.

Hannah touched her scar again. The points on her neck where he had bitten her … they were numb. She had lost them. She shivered and drew in her knees. She had been under his spell then. She would have done anything for him. Would it be the same if he returned? If he came to find her here in England?

Hannah shook her head as if to shake out her thoughts and headed for the shower. As the water worked her memory away, she counted the reasons she was worrying for nothing.

"One," she muttered out loud, "I'm *never* going to see any of them again." "Two," she counted on her fingers, "Jel and Tobias hate me, always did, and will not waste their time looking for me." She wasn't completely sure of that, but listed it anyway.

"Three,"—her voice sounded stronger now—"Bret left me for Tressie." Hannah almost spat the name and then winced as shampoo stung her eye.

It had been another enchanted evening in the Trellis

bar. Jel and Tobias had reluctantly come to play billiards with Hannah and Bret. After a year, Jel and Tobias still didn't particularly like to look at or talk to her. That night, though, they were strangely excited. They kept talking about a woman, a vampire, named Tressie. She had been Bret's fiancée one hundred years before but had left him heartbroken. No one had heard from her since. Bret had told Hannah about his ex-fiancée before. But now there were rumors that she was back in town.

Hannah wasn't worried, even though Jel and Tobias said that once Tressie came back, things would change, and that Bret would of course dump "the human." They had looked meaningfully at Hannah. But Hannah and Bret were hanging out almost nightly now. She felt sure he was over Tressie.

Then a woman walked in. Her figure was long and thin, like a cat's. She was wearing a cape with a velvet collar. And her expression was fierce—and furious. It could only be Tressie, Hannah had thought.

Bret had left Hannah's side immediately. He walked up to Tressie, who merely said, "I'm back, darling," and then grabbed his head and kissed him very coolly. She eyed Hannah as she kissed Bret, and Hannah could only stare in shock. Bret was not resisting, and Tressie was all over him. Jel and Tobias had laughed.

"Little girl"—Tressie's scraping voice came out like nails on a windowpane—"If he is not yet tired of you, he would have been soon. I'm doing you a favor."

Hannah had looked pleadingly at Bret, who would not look up from the floor. Tressie came up close—too close. Her breath smelled awful, like blood or something decaying. Tressie whispered, close to Hannah's face, "I should eat you now. But I don't have a taste for stupid girls. I hope you don't sleep too deeply. I might change my mind. Watch out for me."

Then Tressie's cold yellow eyes settled on the necklace around Hannah's neck. She had hissed, "This is mine," and pulled at the necklace chain. It broke, leaving red marks on Hannah's neck. Tressie's clawlike hand snatched the pearl necklace, her long nails scraping Hannah's skin. Then Tressie had pushed Hannah against the wall, leaving her back sore for days. She could hear Jel and Tobias laughing in the background. Tressie's cartoonish, skeletal grin had exposed her sharp, fanglike teeth, and Hannah had actually whimpered. She remembered it well.

But what had really hurt more than the snatched necklace—Hannah's prize possession gone—more than the fear of meeting Tressie again, was Bret's nonchalance. He had stood watching the floor in the far corner of the room and had made no move to stop Tressie. When she took the necklace, when she had Hannah against the wall—nothing. When Tressie swept out of the room, Bret left with her. Left Hannah as her heart broke. She crumpled onto the floor, massaging the red marks on her neck and crying—for how long? She still didn't know. It could have been hours.

Remembering Bret's monotonous stare, those green eyes looking not at her, but at the floor, as if he didn't see what was happening, Hannah began to sob in the shower, her tears mixing with the running water. After a few minutes, she shouted, "Ridiculous!" and rubbed her eyes. She had cried enough over him. She turned off the water, toweled off, and dressed in a pair of warm fleece pajamas from her aunt. She went to the kitchen, poured a bowl of cereal, and made another cup of steaming hot chocolate. There, she waited at the little plastic table for morning, listening to a branch scraping eerily against the window. Disturbingly, it reminded her of Tressie's metallic voice. She hoped the sun would make an appearance in the morning.

Chapter 5 – Mr. Heartbreak

"So, what happened to you today?" Lily asked in the White Otter pub that evening over their second pint of apple cider. Lily, Hannah, and four other girls were seated quite close together in a booth in the corner. Hannah was staring listlessly out the window, wondering if the rain would ever stop.

"Huh?" Hannah turned her attention back to the table. Lily had been talking to the other girls but was now focused on Hannah. Hannah realized she had been paying less attention to the conversation than she had thought.

"Sorry," Hannah apologized and then laughed as Lily comically waved her hand back and forth across Hannah's downcast eyes.

"Well, where were you? You look sad."

"Um … just thinking about *him* … the guy from the past. Well, I guess because I'm going home in a month," Hannah admitted.

"Ah, Mr. Heartbreak," Lily nodded sagely. "Tell me about him—you never talk about him."

"Well," Hannah replied, "It's boring, really. I mean, old story, right? We went out for a year. Then his old girlfriend turned up and stole him back." Only Hannah didn't tell Lily how old the old girlfriend was.

"Really?" Lily's eyes widened. "Stole him from you? What did she have that you don't have?"

"History," Hannah replied, tucking a leg underneath her. "They used to go out for ages. They were even engaged ... once."

"And you didn't fight for him?" Lily asked. "Demand she leave the scene, I mean, if you had been dating a whole year?"

"Well ... " Hannah looked down. "She is a lot stronger than me."

"Stronger ..." Lily leaned in to peer at Hannah's face. "You mean, she beat you up?"

"Yeah, a little," Hannah admitted.

"God! What a witch!" Lily exclaimed.

"Exactly," Hannah fervently nodded.

"Is that where you got those scars?" Lily asked, pointing to her neck. "I always wondered what it was. Tiny, but it looks like a nasty gash."

"Yeah. Glass," Hannah invented. It was easier than explaining the whole thing, and besides, Lily would never believe her.

"You poor thing!" Lily hugged her tightly. "No wonder you were on a no-boy policy!"

"Do you know the funny thing?" Hannah suddenly exclaimed. "It wasn't anything to do with that ... girl ... that really hurt. I mean sure, she was nasty and I was scared of her. But what really hurt was Bret, the guy, he watched all this stuff happen and he never defended me. He didn't step in, he just let her ... hurt me and ... he acted like he didn't care! But he used to, he used to,"

Hannah's voice shook. "How can I trust another guy, really trust him, when my closest friend just let her take my necklace, and let her beat me up … and he … he just watched …"

Hannah came close to losing it, and started to sniffle.

Lily quickly patted her shoulders. "You need a scotch."

When Lily came back with the drinks, Hannah took a deep breath, smiled weakly in thanks, and took the shot glass.

"Men," Lily admitted. "They become spineless at moments like those. I'm sure he still cared, but he probably, well … something like that happened to me."

"To you?" Hannah asked, taking a sip of the scotch and feeling immediately warmer. She focused on Lily's flushed cheeks and listened.

"Yup. My first year here. Before I met Mr. Rich," Lily waved her hand and her ring flashed. "He was so nice, always taking me to picnics—he would make these gorgeous meals, sandwiches, strawberries, champagne, everything, and he would find the most lovely spots along the river … " a misty expression stole over Lily's face, and Hannah's face echoed it, imagining a younger, bigger-eyed Lily having sandwiches with a young man on a picnic blanket in the sun.

"And then?" Hannah asked, shaking them both out of the reverie. Lily's face snapped back into her normal expression, perhaps a bit colder.

"Mummy didn't approve. Mummy found a better match. Someone the family knew. And bam! Just like that. No more Lily."

"Gosh, that's awful," Hannah lamented into her now empty glass.

"Spineless."

"That happened your first year in Cambridge?" Hannah asked.

"Yup, I had just started university. I really wanted to leave after that, but you know," Lilly shrugged, "it's a good place to study. And then my third year here, he came along … " Lily pointed at the ring. "I decided to do my postgrad studies here."

Hannah chewed her lip. "That's sad, I'm sorry," she lamented.

Lily waved cheerfully at a figure by the door. "No, it's all right. I mean, it *is* sad, but I found Mr. Rich. Tom. And I do trust him. I didn't think I could, either. But he was so lovely and sure. It was just so easy to trust him."

Then she winked. Hannah squinted to make out a waving figure coming toward the table. She recognized Matthew when he was inches away from her face, studying her. He was wearing a colorful, striped scarf that brought out the blue in his eyes. Devastating, Hannah thought, and then bit her lip. She hadn't said that out loud, had she?

"What's happened to this one, then?" Matthew asked Lily, winking. "Too much of the sauce?"

Hannah noticed the other girls at the table staring at Matthew hopefully. Yes, he did look dashing tonight, she reasoned; it was not only the scotch talking. Then she put her hands to her head. "No men. No men," she mouthed silently.

"This lady," Lily said dramatically, waving the empty scotch glass, "needs an escort to take her home. Are there any gentlemen willing to accept the task?" Lily looked pointedly toward Matthew.

Hannah tried to say, "Let him at least have a drink," but the words wouldn't come.

Matthew offered his arm to Hannah. "Shall we?" he asked.

As Hannah reached for her coat, Lily threw her arm around Hannah's shoulder and whispered in her ear, "The best cure for love is love." Then she pushed Hannah out of the booth and into Matthew's waiting arm. Hannah had to catch his arm to stabilize herself. Though she wobbled, she made it to the pub door, leaning on Matthew more than she wanted to. His arm, it is so strong, she thought. And she could feel the warmth emanating through his coat. Focus, she reminded herself.

"Wow," he remarked as he helped her put on her coat, just before going outside. "Looks like someone had too much fun." Hannah kept missing the armhole of her coat.

Hannah laughed and joked, "Not yet! Not nearly enough!" and the tiny voice in her mind saying, "No! Don't trust him! No!" fell silent.

As soon as they stepped out into the cold night, Hannah felt her eyesight clearing and her step growing steadier. It had stopped raining. She still held onto Matthew's arm, but more companionably than for balance, now.

"See, you just needed a little fresh air," Matthew grinned. "You feel all right?"

Hannah nodded and looked up at the moon. The last time she had seen the moon was months ago in San Francisco. Now look how my life has changed, she thought. She was walking in the dark night without any fear, with a devastatingly cute, kind boy by her side. She had spent the whole evening with friends, and felt lighter, having shared her story of the breakup with Lily, and in turn hearing Lily's story. She felt lucky.

"Wow, what it must have been like with smoke!" Hannah remarked, thinking back to the pub. "I mean, the air was already stuffy. I wish I could see a real smoke-filled pub one day." She absentmindedly leaned against Matthew.

He nodded. "It's true, they don't feel the same without smoke. And look, you … " he took a deep breath of her hair, "… you still smell like you! Not smoke. Very strange."

Hannah giggled. They had already reached the tall wooden door of her brick college house.

"Wow," she remarked. "That was quick. We're already here." She leaned against the brick wall by the door and stared up at Matthew. She had a sudden urge to throw her arms around his shoulders and kiss him. She giggled nervously.

"Now, plenty of water," Matthew laughed and shook an admonishing finger at her.

"Right … or plenty of coffee. Would you like one?" Hannah asked. Matthew looked surprised but then nodded. "Okay, if you're sure you're all right." They climbed the green, carpeted stairs to the communal kitchen. Hannah was glad to see that none of the other students who shared the house were around. She directed Matthew to an empty chair.

The kitchen was not much to speak of. Its bare walls and single table were more functional than cheerful, and the plastic cabinet covers didn't quite fit over the cabinets, causing them to remain partially open and askew. Normally, Hannah found this kitchen sterile and a little sinister. One window looked out over the tiny street below. It was a dark alleyway, and a tree grew from the sidewalk, breaking it up with its roots. The limbs reached all the way to the window, where they made a scraping sound if the wind blew them against the glass. As Hannah watched Matthew trying to sit comfortably in the little plastic chair, shifting his long legs into an awkward position under the table, the kitchen suddenly seemed more cheerful.

She smiled as she moved around the kitchen assembling the coffeemaker.

"You recover quickly," Matthew commented.

"To be honest, I never drank that much before!" Hannah admitted. Just as she thought she had gotten her body under control, the coffee filters came crashing down over her head as she attempted to lift them off a high shelf.

"I stand corrected," Matthew joked and reached across her for the filters. He switched places with her, maneuvering her gently into the chair. He quickly finished making the coffee, and they drank it, making small talk about their Christmas plans.

The coffee made Hannah feel more clearheaded, but her eyes, against her will, began to close.

"I think it's time for the princess to turn back into a pea. Or something like that," Matthew said gently.

Hannah laughed. "Yes, I think sleep is calling me."

She saw Matthew to the door, where they hugged in parting. Still in each other's arms, neither made a move to leave. A little voice in Hannah's mind whispered, "Do it. Kiss him." She lifted her face toward his. Seeing his eyes so close to hers sent a nervous thrill through her body. She pressed her lips against his, and he kissed her back.

Soft, Hannah thought. His lips were soft. When they broke apart, Matthew squeezed her arms and then said "Good night" in a low, husky voice. He winked and then walked away. It was of Matthew that Hannah dreamed that night—nice, easy dreams involving picnics by the river in the sun.

Chapter 6 – The Necklace

For the next two weeks, Hannah did not dream about Bret at all. Her dreams and waking life were filled with biology classes, scouring the library for books for her master's thesis, and the great, great surprise of Matthew. They saw each other every day, either for coffee, drinks, or dinner. Hannah had finally bought a thick, warm coat that reached to her knees. She could now face the wintry air with no qualms. They took long walks along the river and even talked about the future together. There were so many things they could do, Hannah realized, that she could never have done with Bret. Matthew wanted to show her his hometown up in Yorkshire. He described how beautiful the hill country was, especially in summer.

"Lucky you, you could meet my family!" Matthew joked, but Hannah saw the sincerity in his face. She imagined two jolly people with bright eyes like their son's. Whereas Bret's parents were long gone; she could never know his family. On one of their walks, Matthew nervously asked her if she was thinking of having children one day.

"Yes," she answered, and he relaxed. Wow, she thought,

never having imagined she would be with someone who thought so far into the future. With Bret, it was more about the moment, or, if anything, the past.

She felt so connected to Matthew that it was difficult to say good-bye for Christmas.

"It's just two weeks," Hannah said, staring into her coffee mug. They were seated in her kitchen again, as her housemates had already left for the break. "But it seems so far away."

"We'll e-mail," Matthew said supportively. "And I'll ring you Christmas Day."

"Call," Hannah murmured against his shoulder. "In the States you call, you don't ring."

"In the U.S., you mean," Matthew laughed.

Hannah suddenly turned serious. "I'm… nervous about going home," she admitted.

"Because of the biting man?" Matthew asked.

Hannah nodded. Matthew took her chin in his hand, and raised her face to his.

"Listen," he explained. "You don't have to be afraid. Just tell him you're with me. Better yet, don't meet with him at all."

Hannah nodded. "I don't plan to meet with him. But what if he comes to find me?" she asked nervously.

"Then tell him you've moved on, and that you have a new life," Matthew soothed.

Hannah nodded again. "Anyway, he probably won't turn up. He doesn't even know I'm coming back for Christmas," she reasoned.

Matthew started to dig through his backpack. He found a small package, and placed it into Hannah's hand. "Just so you don't forget me … I wanted to give you this," he said, and smiled.

Hannah looked at the small box wrapped in Christmas paper she was now holding.

"Oh my gosh," she said nervously. "I mean … I totally didn't know we were exchanging gifts before the holidays … "

Matthew laughed. "You just sound like, so California. Is that what you're going to sound like when you get back?" He kissed her forehead. "I love it."

Hannah laughed too. "I was going to get you something in the States. I mean the U.S." She looked up at Matthew apologetically.

"No, don't worry. I saw this and thought of you. I had to get it."

"Okay. I'm done feeling guilty now!" Hannah proceeded to rip open the paper.

"Whoa, girl!" Matthew exclaimed as he watched Hannah quickly disassemble the package. She opened the box and froze. A necklace sat in the box. The golden chain held a pearl encased in gold leaves.

"You just look like a pearl person," Matthew explained as he gently lifted the shining necklace out of the box and fastened the clasp behind her neck. His hands were warm—warm and soft. "There …" he stepped back. "Perfect."

"It's, um … gorgeous," Hannah managed to say. And it was. Two delicate light gold leaves encased the little pearl that shone in the sunlight coming through the kitchen window.

"But how did you know … did Lily say something?" Hannah asked.

"About what?" Matthew asked, and his forehead

creased in puzzlement.

"Oh, just that I ... lost a favorite necklace once," Hannah explained. Anyway, she was pretty sure she had never described the necklace to Lily. The similarity to the necklace Bret had given her was uncanny.

"Well, now you have another! Don't take it off until I see you again. That way you won't forget me," Matthew said half-jokingly, kissing her hand.

Hannah wacked him on the arm with a glove. "Of course I won't forget you M ... M ... what was your name again?"

Hannah left the necklace on. It gave her courage. She lay in bed in her clothes. She planned to sleep just a few hours and then jump out of bed and brush her teeth in order to catch the five o'clock coach to the airport. Such an early flight, but she would have a long stopover in New Jersey, so she wouldn't land until five at night, San Francisco time. Suddenly, Hannah wondered if it would be dark when she landed. Five o'clock ... would it be dark yet? She couldn't remember. As she drifted to sleep, she fingered the necklace. It reminded her of Matthew, only Matthew, and she was grateful to have someone like him, so soon after moving to England. "But why," an annoyed voice complained in her mind, "why did it have to be pearl?"

Chapter 7 – When They Met

During the long plane ride to San Francisco, Hannah looked through the photo album she had made of her life in Cambridge. Most of the pictures in the first half were of King's College. Matthew played a starring role in the second half of the album. Hannah had not yet told her mother or aunt about Matthew, but she knew that it was time to. It looked like they were staying together at least during the break, and, she hoped, much longer. Hannah knew they would love him. Matthew was kind, respectful, a good student—every parent's dream. She fingered her necklace and pictured what her dad would say. He would probably say, "It's great to know someone's looking after you all the way out there in England." He had been worried about her moving so far away from home.

Of course, she hadn't been safe at home, and her parents and aunt knew it. They had never met Bret, and she hadn't told them she was seeing him the whole year they were together. Bret had met her near school, at bars and nightclubs or movie theaters—dark places. Bret had an uncanny ability to find her; he would emerge from a shadowed corner during a spontaneous trip to the mall.

She couldn't take him home, though they had dated for a year. His face was too pale, his eyes were too hypnotic; he couldn't pass for human, not really.

When Tressie came on the scene with her threats, and when Bret's gang decided she knew too much about them, she had realized she had to tell her parents something. Why she wouldn't go out alone, why she stayed home all night. She told them a lie—that she had been seeing a boyfriend who had turned violent. But this was not the truth; in fact, Bret was the only one of the vampires she didn't fear. It had felt good to unburden her fears to her family, even if they didn't know the full story (how could they?). Then the scholarship to Cambridge came through, and she hadn't hesitated before accepting. To get far away ...

After that night of the breakup, Hannah reflected, fingering Matthew's necklace again, it was Tressie she had most feared. She had not slept well for two weeks, waiting for those long fingernails to rake against her throat again. Every girl with dark, curly hair sent her heart into a panicked beat. But she never saw Tressie after that night. Or Bret. Perhaps, Hannah thought, Tressie had left her alone because she hadn't considered her much of a rival. Hannah had to admit this was true. Not against a vampire.

It was Jel and Tobias who turned out to be the ones to fear. They had never liked the fact that she knew all their locations and hangouts—even their weak points. Now that she was without Bret's protection, they had no hesitations. They had talked about "doing away with the girl" as soon as there were rumors that Tressie had come back to town, and they were thrilled when Tressie finally returned. They couldn't enter her house—Hannah had never invited them in, unlike Bret. But for weeks they stalked her, from the corner outside her house. They were there at night, and on foggy days. They just waited at first, then tried tricks to get Hannah to come outside. They once stole her friend Cindy's cell phone and called Hannah using Cindy's voice, asking her to help, saying her car had broken down. Hannah had called Cindy's landline to find her safe at home. Hannah shuddered to think what would have happened if she had believed it. She pulled the blue airplane blanket up closer to her chin.

Hannah had to tell her parents something, so she said that Jel and Tobias were Bret's friends, positioned to make sure Hannah wasn't seeing anyone else. She convinced her parents not to call the police, since she didn't want any ugly mix-ups between policemen and the vampires. Hannah hoped Jel and Tobias would eventually lose interest and stop haunting the corner. They were there for months, however—up until the day Hannah left for England. Weeks ago, her mom had mentioned that "those strange men, Bret's friends" had stopped hanging out on the corner. Hannah figured they might even have left town by now. She did know a lot about them, and, while she couldn't exactly call the police (what would they be able to do? and they would never believe her anyway) the vampires would probably feel safer in a new town.

Hannah tried to watch a movie on the tiny screen in front of her, but she couldn't concentrate. She leaned her head against the little window of the plane and drifted into a dream …

She dreamed of the day she and Bret had met. The sun had been shining that day, and Hannah and her university friends had gone to the beach. She had gotten a lot of sun, which gave her skin a golden hue. She had always tanned quickly, and her skin was warm, glowing. They had decided to go to their favorite bar, the Regal, for cocktails. It seemed to fit after a long day at the beach. She had a piña colada, and the music had a live, jazzy beat. She tasted the coconut in her dream. Her friends laughed, and she noticed a boy in the corner. He looked sad in the shadows. Feeling Hannah's eyes on him, he looked up. He stared into her eyes, and even from that distance, they seemed full of light.

In a second—too fast—he was by her side.

"Can I taste that?" he asked and she nodded, strangely unable to speak. He took a sip, and immediately his nose wrinkled. "Ugh… so sweet." She watched his nose wrinkle, and when he sneezed, she broke up into peals of laughter.

"You never had a piña colada?" Hannah asked.

"Um, no … " He now looked sheepish. "I never thought of trying one. I didn't think I would like it." His voice was enchanting. Clear, and softly accented. Was he French? German? She couldn't tell. She felt mildly dizzy.

"So, you thought you'd try mine?" Hannah asked teasingly. She tried not to look at her friends, who were giving her thumbs-up signals.

"Well," he leaned in to whisper into her ear, "if a beautiful girl straight from the sun can't make it taste good, no one can." He smiled then, and his emerald eyes swam and flashed with light. Hypnotic, she decided, as her knees wobbled.

"I miss the sun," he then whispered unexpectedly, touching her arm. A chill flashed up her arm. She shivered.

"But," Hannah barely found the words to speak; her heart was racing. She could feel her cheeks flush red, and she was glad the bar was dark so he couldn't see. "It was sunny all day," she managed to say.

"I avoid the sun. Skin condition," he whispered. "Dance with me." They were so close they were almost dancing anyway. He took her piña colada and placed it on the bar.

"Get rid of this, please?" he asked with his eyebrows raised. She laughed again and they danced, so close, so hypnotic … she went home in a daze.

Hannah woke up with a small gasp, her head pressed up against the plane window. Outside, it was sunny. As sunny as that day. She sighed. A whole year with him, and it had been one dizzy dance after another. They had intoxicated each other. She had learned, disturbingly, that it was she he had wanted to taste on the straw, not her cocktail. He had seriously thought about taking her out the back way and drinking her then, but she had come with friends.

Killer, she had thought, when he confessed the story of their initial meeting to her. But at that point, four months into their relationship, it was too late. She didn't care.

"I feed once a month," he had confessed in his soft, lilting voice.

"On girls?" she had yelped.

He had shrugged. "Anyone." But she wasn't convinced that that was true. He was always noticing young girls in their twenties, Hannah's age. Still, she could not break away from him; she needed to see him. She shivered now to think of this. He was a killer.

She clutched her necklace and closed her eyes once again, willing herself to dream of Matthew. She pictured his blue eyes, his easy smile. She smiled and drifted off to sleep …

… and dreamed of the first night she knew what Bret was, when they were alone together in a mansion. Bret had brought her there during a full moon. He claimed it was the house of a distant relative, though Hannah learned later that he had broken in. Hannah had been amazed at the house. The long, arcing stairs from the foyer were marble. They had talked on those grand stairs for a long time and then made their way to a fragrant and lush garden filled with flowering plants that perfumed the air, and white marble statues, glinting in the moonlight. They had sat at the foot of one of the statues in the garden. It was the statue of a Greek god, muscles and face sculpted perfectly. They had talked as the moon rose higher, lighting their faces. She had held his hand.

It was strange how, all of a sudden, she had realized it. A month of meeting in dark bars and movie theatres had not hidden the fact that his eyes swam with light and his strength was far beyond that of anyone she had known. He seemed to know her thoughts. He could find her in a crowd, turned as soon as she walked into a room. And his face … so white and sculpted, but almost too thin. And his hand, she held it now—it was cool, not warm, and not exactly soft, either. A month earlier, they had gone Goth dancing at a club in San Francisco, and he had fit right in. Pale skin, dark hair, dark jacket. Only his eyes looked … she had to admit it … alive.

His eyes betrayed him, in the end. They moved, they flashed, they hypnotized her with light. She became dizzy if she stared into them too long. And, despite his youthful face and body, they looked old. As if they stared out from years ago.

She was so dizzy; they had just kissed in the moonlight, and she held his hand and looked into his face, full of light from the moon. Then she looked at the statue just above them. The moon glinted off the marble just as it glinted off Bret's skin. Hannah suddenly realized that Bret could not be human, and he must have sensed it. His eyes grew wary.

"What are you?" she had whispered. But she had felt no fear.

He had closed his eyes. Later, she learned that they never allowed a "victim" who had learned the truth to live. This was to be her last question. But he had loved her too much to give her up … then.

"Do you really want to know?" he had asked, with his eyes closed. In Hannah's dream, he sounded tired, his voice barely audible.

Hannah nodded, and his eyes were closed, but he knew she had assented. So he smiled. Wider. And she saw his fangs. He took her hand and pulled it to his chest, under his shirt. There was no heartbeat. He took his pocketknife and cut his finger. There was no mark.

"Vampire?" she had asked, the word sounding all wrong, a sacrilegious thing to call her love.

"You can call us that," he had reluctantly agreed. "How I miss the sun," he lamented, and now she could hear years of longing in his voice.

"How old …" she asked breathlessly.

"I'm very old. More than one hundred years," he said, "but I am also young, like you. I was turned when I was eighteen. I still have many of the feelings I did then, 135 years ago. Yes, some of the same desires." He traced her lips with his finger then. He considered.

"You are not afraid?" he asked hesitantly.

"Of you?" she asked. She thought. "A little." She considered again. "No." She traced his lips with her finger. They were soft and cool.

He thought for a moment—a long moment. Then he suggested something. "Meet the rest of us. My family."

"Your family? Like, parents?"

Bret shook his head. "Long gone. No, the others who walk at night. We are three in my family."

She had agreed, curious. She had thought they would be accepting, welcoming. She had been wrong. They were so angry that Bret had led her to their home. When she was introduced to Jel and Tobias, they had hardly looked at her. Hannah thought they looked sinister, nothing like her Bret. Their skin was too tight across their faces, and their eyes were a piercing yellow. Screaming between the three followed. They argued with Bret, wanted to kill her right then. Hannah snuck to a shadowy corner and crouched down low.

The tall one, Tobias, had looked over from the next room and his voice rang out, "Do you think I don't see you there, girl?" Hannah shook, and she shook in her dream again.

Bret's higher voice rang out, bell-like, "I love her. I won't let her go."

Those were the words in Hannah's mind when she

woke up. So Jel and Tobias let me live, not wanting to upset Bret, she thought. And then Bret betrayed his own words and let her go. And afterward, Bret had left her to die in the hands of those fiends. No, Hannah thought to herself. He never loved me.

Hannah was still unsure why Jel and Tobias hated her so. It was true, she knew their hiding places and secrets. But even when she herself wanted to become a vampire, they were against it. Bret had brought up the subject one night over the billiards table, and Tobias had immediately spat out, "She knows nothing." The words rang in her mind. "She is too young to be turned. She would be a burden." Jel had nodded in agreement with Tobias.

"I was eighteen when I was turned," Bret had answered.

She could still see the scene. Tobias, his long body curved like a comma as he shouted, shaking the pool cue. Jel, his dark hands pleading with Bret, asking him to drop the subject. None of them bothered to look at her.

"Please, let's just play without fighting. And look how reckless you turned out! If you had been turned later, you would not be so impulsive!" Jel had argued.

Tobias had been more firm. "It is against our rules. You will both be cast out, and we will hunt you both, if you turn the girl."

"But I love her," Bret had pleaded. "I want to be with her forever." Anguish had laced his voice. But now Hannah considered whether it had really been anguish. Maybe she had just been a passing fancy for him. If he loved her so much, and he couldn't imagine life without her, how could he have let Tressie abuse her? And then gone away with Tressie, leaving Hannah for the fiends?

Hannah shook her head to free it of these thoughts. It had worked out the best for her in the end, she mused. What if she had been turned? She would still be in Jel and Tobias's pack, as she thought of it. There would be so much fighting. There would be no Christmas at home, no more coffees with her aunt. And no Matthew … she clutched the necklace.

She had been stupid. So stupid. It had not been love; she had been under Bret's spell. But his eyes … she had felt such peace when she met his gaze. So protected when he held her hand. Suddenly Hannah's palms turned clammy. What was she doing, coming to San Francisco? She was putting everyone in danger, including herself. She should have gotten her parents and aunt to come to England, instead. She should never have agreed to come home for Christmas.

They were landing in thirty minutes. And would it be dark? She was relieved to see that it would be four thirty, an early arrival. It would definitely still be light. They would go straight home. Hannah breathed. Even if Tressie, Jel, or Tobias was waiting for her, she would be safe enough if she stayed indoors at night.

As the plane started its descent, Hannah tried to put aside her fears and focus on seeing her family again. She flipped through the photo album and wondered what Lily and Matthew were doing now. She was so excited to tell her family about Matthew. She breathed easier to think that she would see her parents in just half an hour or so. Maybe her aunt would even be there, waiting for her at the airport. She convinced herself that she was relaxed and ready to present a happy face for her family. Then, she noticed with dismay that she was clutching her necklace so tightly it had made a mark on her palm.

Chapter 8 – Homecoming

Once Hannah had shown her passport, answered the questions of the customs officer, and dragged her heavy suitcase full of tea and other gifts from England off the moving belt, she felt calmer. This was real life. This was something she recognized. Her arms and legs felt cramped from sitting on the plane, and she stretched. Then she took a deep breath, trying to shake off the fog of the long flight, and walked through the exit.

A high-pitched scream reached her ears, but she was slow to react. After all, in England it was one in the morning. She blinked and then saw her mom in a red floral shirt. It looked new, Hannah thought. Her dad stood next to her mother, grinning. The scream came again, and Hannah realized it was her mom screaming her name! They started to wave frantically with joy as Hannah gave a meek smile to the group. Her mom, dad, and aunt all held a big sign, saying, "Welcome Home, Hannah." Geez, thought Hannah, smiling more broadly now. What would it have been like if she had actually been away for a year? There would have been fireworks!

Hannah barely had time to set down the heavy suitcase when she was enveloped in a big hug. Each of them hugged her in turn, and when they released her, they all said she looked great. Hannah didn't believe them, after the long flight. She knew she must look tired. Then again, the last time they had seen her was during those awful months when she had been stalked by vampires … she had probably looked worse then. Now she smiled and said she had been sleeping well in England. Her father looked relieved and hugged her again.

Her aunt Laura noticed the necklace within minutes.

"Is that a new necklace, dear? It suits you." Hannah nodded, smiling. "Is it a gift from someone special?" her aunt asked, searching Hannah's face. Hannah nodded again, and her Aunt's face broke out into a glowing smile.

"But … " her mom said, confused, "didn't you have one like that before? You know, you told me you had bought it at a vintage shop."

Hannah shook her head. "I had one like it, but I … the chain broke, and I lost it. It was just a cheap replica. The funny thing is, Matthew didn't know what it looked like. Actually, it's just a coincidence that he picked a similar pattern!"

Her mom and aunt looked at each other, mouthing, "Matthew?" Suddenly, Hannah was pelted from all sides with questions. As they made their way to the car, her mom asked what he looked like. Hannah showed her a picture of Matthew after he had just gone running. He was smiling, and his cheeks were flushed. Her mother grabbed the little book Hannah had made and eagerly flipped through the pictures, her father pleading with her to slow down so he could see them better. Her aunt asked all about Matthew—how old he was, what he liked to do for fun. Her father asked what he was studying. Hannah was almost hoarse by the time they reached the car.

While they lingered by the vehicle, Hannah suddenly realized how dark the parking lot was. Her heart began to race, and she felt dizzy. Her aunt asked her what was the matter.

"Jet lag, long flight, I'm okay. I just need to get home," Hannah mumbled. Her parents and aunt all exchanged glances.

"Honey…" her father started to ask and then hesitated. Her mom shot him a warning glance, but he continued. "Does … *he* … know you're back?"

Hannah understood the question immediately. "No," she said with confidence, though she couldn't be certain. He had always seemed to know where she was before … before he ran off with Tressie.

"Well, then," her aunt broke into a grin. "There's nothing to worry about! We'll have a nice, peaceful Christmas."

"We decided to take a trip up the coast for New Year's!" Her mom smiled with delight as she delivered this news. Hannah felt the tension in her own face lighten. A trip! Why hadn't she thought to suggest that? A trip away was a safe option, a great idea. She silently kicked herself when she realized that they could have all met in San Diego for the holidays, or Florida—somewhere warm. Her family would have understood her reluctance to return. Oh well, Hannah thought. Next time. She felt better knowing they would be traveling for the holidays. Still, she realized she had been holding her breath until they climbed into the car, and the doors were all locked.

Then she could relax.

On the way home, Hannah was flooded with more questions. "Was it very cold when you left? How did you meet Matthew? What's Lily doing for the holidays?" Hannah didn't even have a chance to ask what her parents and aunt had been up to for the last few months.

It was sunset when they got to the house. Hannah breathed with relief as she and her family reached the familiar blue door of the two-story house with bay windows that was home. The living room hadn't changed at all, Hannah could see. The green sofa looked just as inviting, plush, and comfortable, with a Mexican blanket lying across it, inviting someone to curl up and read a book. The fireplace was hardly ever used, but Hannah had some great memories of warm evenings in front of a crackling log, talking to her parents or warming her feet in front of the fire.

Her mother had made lasagna, Hannah's favorite dinner, and she felt her mouth watering as soon as she smelled the tomato and basil in the air.

By the time they ate dinner, opened Hannah's first gifts of tea and Cadbury's chocolates (there were more gifts to come on Christmas Day), and then looked through Hannah's album ten times, she was exhausted. She had to beg to be released from story-telling, and they agreed to let her sleep. As Hannah climbed the carpeted stairs to her room, her mother informed her that her friend Cindy had called. Cindy was expecting Hannah to visit in the next few days, to say hi.

"And the girls want to see you," she said, smiling, meaning Hannah's three friends from university, the ones who had taken Hannah to the bar where she had met

Bret.

Hannah nodded and yawned, only vaguely taking in the information. She groggily agreed to call Cindy the next day. Hannah changed into her pajamas and sank thankfully into her bed, hardly noticing the new flowery comforter (an early Christmas gift from her parents). She realized, just before sinking into sleep, that she had thought of his name, Bret's name, without cringing.

She had Matthew. She had her parents and aunt. She didn't need anyone else.

Chapter 9 – Christmas Eve

The next morning, Hannah woke up at 7:00 AM. Her face was turned to the window, and the strongest ray of sun that she had seen in a long time was shining on her face. She stretched and smiled to see the familiar peach walls of her room and the stuffed elephant from her childhood sitting happily on her wardrobe. She quickly got dressed and made coffee and then went outside into the back garden. Her parents were still sleeping. She sat on the edge of the patio and stared at the morning sky, blinking at the brightness. She didn't want to look away from the warm rays of sun, even when her eyes started to tear.

She spent the first day with her parents and her aunt. They walked along Fisherman's Wharf, just like tourists. Hannah bought a sourdough bread bowl filled with hot clam chowder, and her family bought sandwiches. They ate by the sea, listening to the barking sea lions nearby.

The plane-induced cramps in her legs eased from all the walking. When they got home in the late afternoon, Hannah was exhausted. The jet lag was catching up with her. She called Cindy and only vaguely followed the conversation. They made plans to meet up in a few days.

After two days, she felt warmed and recharged. She no longer needed to be outside at every possible moment. She had already done the things she missed. She had eaten clam chowder, and she had gazed out on San Francisco Bay. The accents and word choice around her were so familiar, it relaxed her. She didn't have to think about what words to use in conversations. Her mom took her shopping at the mall, and she remembered every store; nothing had changed. It would be Christmas tomorrow. And she felt utterly at home.

On the evening of the twenty-fourth, Hannah sat on the floor with her toes as close to the fireplace as possible, her knees pulled up to her chest. Her father had lit a log to celebrate Christmas Eve. He was telling a story of how he and one of his old friends had gone fishing in Oregon and had lost a pole to a giant fish, possibly a shark. Her mom shrieked with laughter as he described how his friend Harry had actually leaped onto a rock, balancing and trying not to lose the pole, which was later pulled out of his hand. Harry was not a graceful man, but apparently he had balanced on one foot for a long while before plunging into the Pacific ocean. They all smiled good-naturedly at the story, especially when her father explained how he then fell in, trying to get Harry out. They had both decided the fish had come out victorious on that trip.

Her aunt was at her own house but would be coming over the next morning with gifts and homemade cookies. And, of course, Hannah felt a thrill when she thought about it: Matthew would call on Christmas Day.

She hugged her knees, feeling chilly despite the fire. Though she had thought she was over the jet lag, after four days, she considered that she might need a few more days to adjust completely. After all, it was ten o'clock San Francisco time, 6:00 AM England time.

"You're on England time now, love." Hannah smiled as Matthew's voice echoed in her mind. After her father was finished telling his story, she got up, stretched, and kissed her parents good night, wishing them Merry Christmas. When she got to her room, she changed into her pajamas and crawled into the bed. But she could not drift off. She suddenly felt awake and alert. The back of her neck prickled.

The moon shone through her window. She wanted to look outside, but she did not, thinking, What if Jel and Tobias were on the corner? What if they were waiting to see whether she had come home for Christmas? She didn't want to give them confirmation by showing her face.

She realized how predictable it was to come home now. She chastised herself. How could she have come here? She had felt so safe in the last four days, but she now wondered whether it had been foolish to feel that way. Her whole family could be in danger, not just her.

She fingered Matthew's necklace, which was still around her neck. It would all be fine, she told herself. She was just being silly. And then a hand covered her mouth.

"Don't scream," a high, lilting voice warned, and the breath that had caught in her chest came out through her nose in a slow "pooof" noise. He lifted his hand away slowly, carefully. The moonlight hit his face, and she could see that it was Bret. But she knew, had known, from his hand, his touch, his voice …

She lay silently on her back, staring at him. Her eyes opened wide. "Haven't you left town?" she finally managed to say.

"Where were you?" he whispered urgently, feverishly. "I tried to find you … for weeks I've been trying."

Hannah stared at him confused. "Why?"

Bret ran his hands through his hair. "Hannah, I …" he took a strand of her dark, straight hair in his hand and ran his fingers through it. "I … made a mistake. Tressie's gone." Now he looked into her eyes, and his own emerald eyes danced.

Hannah felt several things at once. A familiar, dizzy, and warm sensation invaded her senses. She felt that craving to be near him. And she felt disgust. The strong hand that now touched her hair had done nothing to help her while Tressie had abused her. How dare he …

"No," Hannah said firmly. "It's too late."

Bret's eyebrows pulled together. "What do you mean?"

"You stood by and watched her, watched her hurt me!"

"That was not … that was nothing."

"Nothing?" Hannah shrieked, and he put a finger to his lips.

"Shhh," he admonished. Then he stroked her hair, and leaned in to look into her eyes. She didn't move. Couldn't …

But then she could. She looked away, then she sat up. She moved his arm away.

"I couldn't …" he bit his lip. "I know why you are angry. But if I had protected you, she would have killed you then."

"So you acted like … " Hannah asked angrily.

"Yes, I acted. Of course I cared, of course I was worried. And if Tressie knew that, she would not have let you live."

Hannah chewed her lip. It did make sense. But could she have stood by and watched if someone had been hurting Bret? What if someone was hurting Matthew? Matthew, Matthew, Hannah thought. Her hand flew to her necklace, and Bret saw it. He smiled. "Ah, so you found another one. No matter, I have gotten your old one back," Bret put his hand into his shirt pocket and pulled out his great-great-grandmother's gleaming, older golden necklace.

"How …" Hannah asked, confused. "Did you take it back?"

A flicker of something—guilt? pain?—flew across Bret's brow. "Well … sort of."

"Tressie dumped you again, didn't she?" Hannah's voice was strangely flippant.

"Uh …" Bret looked again into her eyes, and reality swam. "She … and I … do not love each other. My heart is yours."

He moved his hand toward her chest again and looked at her with greedy eyes. It was then that Hannah began to feel afraid.

So she made a plan. Anything to delay this meeting.

"Bret," she admitted, "I did not forget you." A look of victory crossed his face. "And I … just had to find this necklace … this reminder …" she played along with his misinterpretation.

"But your goons, they scared me … Jel and Tobias."

Bret looked guilty. "They will not touch you now,"

he promised.

"No, but … I need some time. I need … just a few weeks … to be with my family," Hannah explained.

Bret frowned. "Time?"

"I thought …" and now Hannah's voice betrayed the pain and loss she had felt months ago. "I thought I would never see you again." And she traced his face with her finger, but it was not really his face. It was a face from the past she was seeing, and an old Hannah was touching him. This was a reminder to her. And a good-bye.

But he did not know that. Instead, he grabbed her hand and kissed it. "When, then? How much time? And where did you go? To school?"

"Oh, no … I just went on a trip around America," Hannah lied. "To find myself … again. Now I'm back, and app … applying. But let's meet after the holidays and st … start again." Hannah's heart interrupted her thoughts, and the lie did not come freely. But he seemed convinced. She named the day after her flight, and said she would meet him at their old park. They would catch up then. She warned him that her family was taking a trip for a few days and so not to worry if the house was dark.

Bret leaned down close to her ear and whispered. His breath was cool against her neck. "Until the sixth. Tie up your affairs. We will be together forever. I left Jel and Tobias. There is nothing stopping us from being together." He kissed her then, and Hannah felt a twist of guilt in her heart; his kiss was so different from Matthew's kind one. Matthew's soft one. This kiss was ravenous, greedy, demanding. And her heart raced like a traitor. Then, before she could say anything, or even breathe, he was gone. He was gone, and the window was open.

Hannah was shaking. She leaped out of bed, shut the window, and locked it. Even though it would not keep him out, she felt better. She scanned the night, the corner by her house, with frantic eyes. There was no one there. The road was empty. She tried to slow her breathing down, and crawled back into bed. She had done it. She had convinced him to look for her after the fifth. She would be on a plane to England by the time he looked for her. She had gotten away. Still, Hannah couldn't sleep and instead placed her hand on her neck. It felt cold.

Chapter 10 – Christmas Day

The next morning, the sun shining through Hannah's window woke her at 7:00 AM as usual. She sat up in bed. It was Christmas! she thought, and felt a thrill run through her. Matthew would call! There would be gifts, and her aunt was coming over for brunch. And then, she remembered.

Was it a dream? She looked around the room and gasped. Bret's necklace was draped across her little table. So it was not a dream. She did not want this thing … this thing given to her by a killer who stood by when she was hurt, who hurt her far worse by doing nothing when she was attacked, and then left her, taking away his heart. This shining golden thing had been around the neck of that awful female vampire whose breath smelled of blood. Hannah shuddered and shoved the necklace into the drawer of her bedside table. She touched the necklace around her neck. She thought of it as the good necklace, the innocent necklace.

Hannah went downstairs and started to assemble the coffee machine. At the noise, her mom and then her dad shuffled in, wearing robes and slippers. Both had messy, pineapple-shaped hair. Hannah smiled to see her parents. She wouldn't let the encounter with Bret ruin this precious morning.

Hannah handed each of her parents a mug of coffee, which they sipped gratefully. Then they moved into the living room to open gifts. Hannah received two warm sweaters and some tall black boots with heels.

"I remember you said no one really wears sneakers to walk around in England, so I thought these would keep your feet warm … in style," her mom explained.

Hannah hugged her and said they were perfect.

Her father gave her a book titled, "All about Fenland country, a history of Cambridgeshire and northwards." Hannah said truthfully that it looked interesting.

"This means you have to visit so I can take you on a tour through the fens!" Hannah said, hugging her father.

Then they unwrapped Hannah's gifts of cashmere scarves in tartan patterns. "It's a Scottish style, not English, but I thought you would like them, and they are so soft!" she explained.

The doorbell rang around eleven. It was Aunt Laura with a load of gifts in her arms and a steaming Tupperware full of warm cookies. Hannah helped her put down the packages and quickly crammed two of the chocolate chip cookies into her mouth. They were better than she remembered.

"What do you put in these, Aunt Laura?" Hannah asked. Her aunt only smiled. "I'm glad you like them," she answered.

Aunt Laura had more of a hippie style, in Hannah's eyes, so she had not gotten her aunt a tartan scarf. Instead, she had found a bag from Tibet at the open-air market in Cambridge. Her aunt's eyes opened wide when she unwrapped it. "It's perfect!" she exclaimed. "I love striped bags!"

Aunt Laura's gift to Hannah was a photo frame made of glass cuttings. The glass edges were smooth, and of clear, strong pink and purple colors.

"Did you make this?" Hannah asked, awed. Her aunt nodded.

"I thought you could use it for a picture of new friends, or old." Then she leaned in, grinning. "I guess, though, Matthew will feature."

Hannah nodded. She had already been thinking of which picture of Matthew she would choose.

"Matthew's going to call today!" she told her family.

"All the way from England?" her mom asked.

Hannah nodded, smiling.

She felt happier than ever through the gift-opening and their brunch together. Her mother made potato pancakes, and they almost finished Aunt Laura's cookies. When the phone rang at two, Hannah raced to answer. It would be night in England.

"Matthew," she said when she picked it up.

His beautifully accented voice spoke to her across so many miles.

"So, you remember my name," he joked, and Hannah laughed. She tried to ignore her parents and her aunt, who were still seated at the dining table, watching her.

"Are you with your family?" he asked.

"Yes," Hannah admitted, "and they are listening."

"Well, say 'hello'!" Matthew said, laughing. Hannah passed on the greeting, and held the phone out to her family. They shouted a chorus of "Hi, Merry Christmas!"

at the phone. Hannah held the receiver back to her ear.

Then she yelled out, "He says 'Happy Christmas' back!"

It broke the listening spell, and her parents and her aunt dispersed to give her some privacy.

"Do, did you have a nice morning?" he asked. "And … well, I guess it's still afternoon there!"

"Yes, we opened gifts and had amazing food just now! We'll have to walk it off later!" Hannah gushed.

"And last night? What did you do?" Matthew asked.

Hannah wanted to say "We sat around the fire telling stories," but she couldn't. Her voice caught in her throat. It was Bret she remembered about last night. Suddenly, her hand started to shake. "Um … it was okay. Today is better," she managed. "What about you?"

"What's wrong? You sound odd," Matthew asked, sounding worried.

Hannah nodded but then remembered that Matthew couldn't see her. "Yeah," she admitted, "I'm just a little … worried."

"Is it him? Did you see him again?" Matthew guessed.

"Yes, but I think he's gone now. I told him … a lie. But I think he won't come back looking for me until I've gone."

"Why did you even meet him?" Matthew asked.

Hannah tried not to cry. "He snuck into my room through the window."

"He snuck …" a gasp came on the other end. "Barricade your window."

"I know," Hannah explained, "Now it's locked, but he's clever… he's …"

"Look, I'm coming out there. Someone should be there to protect you. Do your parents know?"

"No!" Hannah almost shrieked, managing to keep her voice down. It would be so much worse with Matthew there. Bret would know the truth instantly, and Matthew would not be safe.

"Look, I'm … I'm going on a trip up the coast with my family. We'll be safe. Bret doesn't know where we're going, or that I'm leaving for England on the fifth."

Hannah managed to calm Matthew down. He promised to try to enjoy the rest of the holiday and not to jump on a plane to California. He, too, would arrive in Cambridge on the fifth, so they would see each other in slightly over a week. He sounded worried, but Hannah promised she would lock the window every night.

As if that could stop Him.

"I'll see you soon," she promised Matthew. "My family loves the necklace you gave me." She could almost hear Matthew smile.

"Tell your family Merry Christmas," Hannah said in closing.

"Okay, but it's 'Happy Christmas' here," he joked, and they said good-bye. But Hannah put the receiver down a little too firmly.

Bret had ruined it. He had ruined her conversation because she was afraid, and Matthew now knew even more than she had wanted him to. And Christmas was tainted.

Because of that killer.

Chapter 11 – Home and England

The trip to Oregon was fantastic. They walked along the foggy coast by day, and listened to jazz music and ate fresh fish by night. And better yet, Hannah felt safe. When they came home on the second, she found she couldn't sleep in her room anymore. She kept feeling that cool breath on her neck and staring nervously at the window. Instead, she dragged her new comforter down to the living room each night and slept on the sofa in sharp spurts. Despite all the food and relaxing days with her family, by the fifth of January, she had purple circles under her eyes. She was actually looking forward to the long flight—nine hours of uninterrupted sleep in a vampire-free zone.

The fifth finally came, with no surprise visits from Bret. Once she had checked in, she had enough time for a last coffee with her family before going through security. As her mom and aunt went to order, her dad maneuvered Hannah toward a little corner table. Her dad looked upset.

"He came back, didn't he?" her dad asked with clenched teeth, once they sat down. Hannah nodded and looked down at her hands.

"Well, next year, we'll meet somewhere else for Christmas. I hate seeing you like this."

Hannah looked up, and a grateful feeling warmed her cheeks.

"Could we? I'm so glad you understand!" she gushed.

For the first time, she noticed her dad looking at the scars on her neck. His expression looked murderous. She was happy she had never introduced her parents to Bret, because she didn't know what her dad would try to do to him. Try … and fail. She shivered. Well, she didn't have to worry now. She wouldn't be at the park when she said she would meet Bret. But what if he came by her house looking for her?

"Dad …" Hannah hesitated, looking at her hands again. "Promise me that if he comes looking for me, don't get angry with him, okay?" She looked up to see a surprised expression on her dad's face. "Just tell him it's over, and that he won't see me again. Tell him I'm far away, but don't tell him where."

"Well … sure, I'll tell him it's over. But I also want to give that creep a piece of my mind …"

"No, Dad, please! He's violent, and I don't want … more trouble. I just want him to go away. He could hurt you … or mom."

Her dad was silent for a moment, his face red. "Well," he conceded. "I can't promise to be nice or even civil. But I won't start a fight."

Hannah winced even to think of her dad picking a fight with Bret. But she told herself that it seemed to be going well. She wouldn't have to come back to San Francisco at all, if she didn't want to. She could see her parents elsewhere. Bret wouldn't know where she had gone and would have to give up.

Once her mom and her aunt returned with four coffees, they spoke about other things. Her mother thrust a gift for Matthew into her hands. It was a San Francisco mug filled with Ghirardelli chocolate and a note saying, "Come visit."

"That's sweet!" Hannah beamed.

They promised to visit England that summer, so it would only be four or five months before they saw Hannah again. At this, her mom threw her arms around Hannah, saying, "Five months! No, it's too long!" But her dad pried her off, promising her the months would fly by, and Hannah promised to call at least once every two weeks and e-mail almost daily.

When Hannah finally left them at the long line through security, she had mixed emotions. She couldn't wait to get back to England and to see Matthew again. She had enjoyed being home, though, and felt a twinge of regret knowing she would not come back to San Francisco any time soon. Still, she sighed, she had gotten away; she was lucky. She fingered her necklace. Her parents and aunt would be coming to Cambridge in the summer, and she could be a happy, relaxed Hannah with them. She knew they worried about her when she couldn't sleep.

One nine-hour flight later, Hannah stumbled off the plane at Heathrow airport in London. She had not slept at all for most of the long flight, but in the last hour she had slipped into a comalike state that she found hard to break out of. She shuffled her way through customs, finding the officer's "Where are you flying from, love?" both strange and familiar. "Love," she had repeated under her breath, hoping she hadn't said it too loudly. Once she extracted her heavy bag from the baggage belt and wandered into the arrivals hall, her eyes scanned for signs pointing her to the coach station. Her eyes caught a friendly, waving arm. She focused on the face and found a pair of familiar blue eyes that appeared to sparkle with diamonds and other bluer gems, and she saw his giant grin.

"Matthew!" Hannah screamed, breaking out of her stupor. She ran to him as quickly as she could, considering the heavy bag, and threw her arms around his neck and shoulders. He enveloped her in a hug, but she suddenly pulled away.

Matthew looked concerned.

"Oh my God! I must smell awful!" she said, alarmed. He laughed and pulled her to him once again.

"You smell fantastic, as always," he said into her hair.

"This is a nice surprise," she said as she looked up into his face.

"Well, I just couldn't wait another two hours. I had to see you immediately." Matthew took Hannah's hand in his and threw the shoulder strap of her heavy bag across his own body.

"Gah! What do you have in here? San Franciscan stones?" he joked.

Hannah laughed. "Well, there's a lot of chocolate in there. Ghirardelli chocolates for you and Lily … and me," she admitted.

Matthew pointed to a little coffee house in the corner of the airport hall. "What do you say we get cappuccinos here and then take the coach back to Cambridge?"

"Sounds wonderful!" Hannah said, feeling more

awake at the idea of a warm cup of coffee.

"What time is it in San Francisco, anyway?" Matthew asked, looking at his watch and furrowing his eyebrows. "Here, it's ten in the morning. So there it's …"

"Uggh!" Hannah groaned. "I don't even want to think about it. The middle of the night!"

"Well, don't get your hopes up about seeing the sun today." Matthew pointed at a gray, rain-slicked window. Hannah had actually thought it was a gray wall. "They say sun in the day helps with jet lag, but I'm afraid it's not happening."

"But you're here," Hannah said, and smiled up at him. "It's such a surprise … really a nice thing to see you just after coming off the plane."

"Does that make up for the crap weather?" Matthew asked.

"Oh, definitely."

"And you're … okay, right? No more … Bret sightings?"

Hannah shook her head no. "No more encounters. Now that I'm here, with you, far from San Francisco, I feel a lot better."

"Well, I'll order those coffees. You sit here. You look tired." Matthew scanned her face.

"I'll be fine," she promised. "Especially after a cappuccino and a giant chocolate cookie."

Matthew saluted her. "Yes, ma'am." Hannah giggled, and he put her bag down near her feet. She maneuvered herself onto a stool. She watched Matthew as he stood in line and ordered the coffees, noting how tall and strong he seemed. The girl at the espresso machine smiled warmly at him. Hannah felt lucky.

When he came back carrying two steaming cups and a big chocolate cookie, he peered at Hannah's face and asked, "What are you thinking?"

"You look great. I mean, you always do. You … you haven't changed," she said.

"Well, it's only been two weeks, love!"

"Well, I mean. It feels like longer," Hannah lamented.

"For me, too," Matthew agreed. "I worried …" he looked down at his coffee, suddenly quiet.

"What?" Hannah prompted. "Were you worried about me?" She rested her hand on his.

"Well, I knew you might see Bret, and I wasn't sure … maybe you would have decided to get back together with him. I … did wonder if you'd still be interested in your polo-playing English chap…"

"Oh Matthew!" Hannah's cheeks flushed. "I'm so lucky to have you! I can't believe how nice it has been, to be with you."

Matthew looked up at her face.

"I feel … seeing you here … I feel like I'm coming home," Hannah said, realizing it was true as she spoke.

Matthew stared into her eyes for a moment and then rested his eyes on her necklace.

"You do really wear that all the time," he said.

"Oh course I do!" Hannah sighed. "How could you possibly doubt my feelings … I mean … Bret was a monster," she shuddered. "Anyway, if I left you I would have to buy a new wardrobe … all my favorite sweaters are now blue. The pearl looks good on blue." Hannah joked.

Matthew smiled. "Okay," he said, seemingly more

relaxed, and he leaned in and kissed her.

Then Hannah remembered something. "Oh! My parents got you something."

Matthew looked on curiously as she pulled out the San Francisco mug and note that she had stuffed in her handbag.

"It's just a little thing, but they wanted you to have this. It's nothing like the necklace, just a silly thing … " Hannah said bashfully.

"Nonsense! I love it! I'll drink from it every morning." Matthew beamed, back to his happy, relaxed self as he read the note. "Come visit, they say! Definitely. Although maybe we could get them to come here, this time?" His eyes danced across Hannah's face with some concern.

"Yes, my dad said the same thing. And, they were talking about coming this summer!"

"Perfect! We can show them Cambridge at its best."

Hannah smiled again to think he was so sure they would be together in the summer, months from now. In fact, she thought, chewing her lip, she hoped they would still be together. She would be devestated if something split them apart.

"You know what?" Hannah said, suddenly serious. "I think I love you." Then she felt her cheeks grow hot. Had she just said that out loud? She had meant it, but she felt so groggy. And the airport café was hardly romantic.

Matthew only stared at her. "Whoa," he said. "I will have to meet you after long plane flights more often." They smiled at each other for what felt like an hour but was only a few minutes.

When they had finished their coffee, Hannah felt awake enough to brave the journey back to Cambridge.

As they walked to the coach station, Hannah held Matthew's hand.

"Thanks again for coming to meet me," she said, gazing into his face.

"I wanted you to be greeted by something good in England … I hope, anyway. Not this rain," he said, gesturing to the window. They were still inside, but Hannah shivered just thinking about walking out of the airport and onto the bus.

"Well, I would say the best part of England has greeted me. And I'm happy to be here," Hannah said meaningfully.

Once they ran through the rain and took their seats on the coach, Hannah felt herself sinking into a calm state. She leaned against Matthew's shoulder and held his hand. She fell asleep for the whole journey, and when she awoke in Cambridge, she felt amazed and lucky to find him still there.

Chapter 12- The First Time

In the next few days, Hannah settled into the routine of classes quickly, though the rain and lack of sun took more getting used to. A few days after her arrival in Cambridge, an e-mail came from her mother saying that a "dark-haired boy came around last night looking for you." Her parents told him she was gone—that she had moved out of the country and would not be back for some time.

Hannah had thought about what she would do if Bret came looking for her. Hannah wrote an e-mail to her mom, attaching a letter for Bret. The letter explained that their time was over, that she had moved on, and so should he. She told her mother to look for the vintage necklace in her nightstand and put it in the envelope. She gave careful instructions to her mom only to deliver the letter and necklace if he came again, but not to look for him. Her mother wrote back immediately that she would do so. She wrote that she was confused about the necklace but wouldn't ask questions if Hannah didn't want to explain.

That night, Hannah told Matthew the whole story of the letter and e-mail. They sat on her bed, their fingers entwined.

But this time, Hannah had something else on her mind. Ever since Matthew had met her at the airport, she had felt more deeply connected to him. Even after she received the e-mail revealing that Bret was still looking for her, Hannah felt safe. She knew that was because of Matthew.

"Are you sad?" Matthew asked her, stroking her face.

"Why? Actually, I was just thinking how happy I am," Hannah responded.

"But ... now you've said good-bye to Bret. I mean formally, officially, with the letter and all. Doesn't it make you ... regret ...?" Matthew asked.

"I regret only that he's still looking for me. I said good-bye to him in my heart before today. This letter was something I had to do, to show him I mean it. But I have moved on from him. I'm not sad at all to have left him behind ... and found you."

Matthew leaned in and kissed her. "Okay." They kissed some more, and then Matthew broke away. He pointed at the clock by her bed but didn't let go of her hand.

"I should probably go," he lamented.

"Or ..." Hannah suddenly felt nervous. "Do you ever feel sad—about Emily, I mean?" she blurted out. She mentally kicked herself. Why did she bring up Emily? She was worried that she had spoiled the mood.

Matthew looked at her with wide eyes. "Why on earth would I miss her?"

"Well, you think I might miss Bret ... I mean ... they are kind of in the same camp ... it's possible, anyway, that you might ..." Hannah broke off as Matthew began smiling and chuckling and stroking her head.

"No, I do not miss her at all. At all!" Matthew smiled. Hannah noticed that he didn't have the sad, reminiscing look on his face that he often had before when Emily came into the conversation.

"Anyway, what camp are you talking about? Emily and Bret …?" Matthew looked slightly confused.

"Monster camp," Hannah admitted, and then Matthew laughed.

"Monster camp! Yeah, you're right, actually." He kissed her one more time and then started to get off the bed. " Okay, if I don't go now, I'm going to sleep here," he said, his eyebrows lifting devilishly.

Hannah stopped him and pulled his arm closer to her. "So, sleep here," she said and kissed him.

He hesitated. "Are you sure?" She nodded vigorously, and he grinned. They started kissing again, but this time more feverishly. Suddenly Matthew broke away.

"Wait … I realized I never told you …" he said as Hannah scanned his face, still close to hers.

"What?" she asked, her heart pounding.

"I love you, too," he murmured and then took her face in his hands and kissed her again.

As Hannah felt the defining lines between them break, she realized she had never felt as safe as she did at this moment. Her heart raced, and then all she knew was a sweet completion she had felt only shadows of before.

Chapter 13 – A Visit to Cambridge

The next weekend, Hannah called home. She wanted to tell her mother what had happened with Matthew, how wonderful it had been. She wasn't sure, however, if her mother would approve; they weren't married, after all. So she decided not to tell her mother about their fantastic night.

Instead, Hannah asked if Bret had come by the house again, and Hannah's mother confirmed that he had.

"He came by and I gave him the letter. He looked confused, dear," her mother reported.

"But you didn't tell him where I am, right?" Hannah asked nervously.

"No. Of course not. Though he really does have a nice smile…"

"No!" Hannah screamed. "It's just an act! Don't fall for it, Mom," Hannah pleaded.

"Okay, okay! I am not saying I like him, knowing what he did to you. Your father didn't like him, anyway," her mother admitted. "Said he looked creepy."

"Creepy. Definitely a creep," Hannah said firmly.

"And how is Matthew?" her mother asked, changing the subject.

Hannah's voice came out dreamy rather than pinched. "Oh, really good. Really great."

She wondered if her mother was smiling or rolling her eyes at Hannah's tone.

"Are you still coming out here to meet him? And to see Cambridge?" Hannah asked.

"Yes, your aunt wants to book the tickets for June. Is that a good time?" her mother asked.

"It's a great time! Matthew will be excited. He loves the San Francisco mug, and he wants to meet all of you!"

Matthew was indeed ecstatic when he heard that "the Hannahs," as he put it, were coming to visit. Even though it was only January, he and Hannah started to discuss the sights that they would show her family. Matthew made a list of the pubs her dad, who liked beer, "needed to see." Hannah wanted to bring them to King's College for cappuccino. They squeezed hands when she said it, because it had been, in many ways, their first date.

"I know why you were on your knees," Matthew had once joked. "It wasn't King's at all. You just had a premonition that a dashing young knight would come sweep you off your feet."

Hannah had laughed. "I wasn't expecting anything like a knight. I got so lucky," she admitted.

The term went quickly, since classes and pub outings with friends kept them busy. On one of the first warm nights in March, Hannah decided to treat Matthew to a late-night picnic of wine and cheese by the river Cam. It was still chilly, but the air had a hint of spring. She wanted to take advantage of the rainless evening. She had a package for him, a little wrapped gift.

Matthew was surprised. "Is it customary to give spring gifts in your land?" he teased.

"No, but I got this lovely necklace from you, and never brought you back a Christmas gift."

"There was all that chocolate you brought. And the stunning mug from your family. I'm going to make good on their invitation you know. Come visit …"

"Yes, but those were silly gifts. This is something I really thought you would like." Hannah forced the package into his hands.

He calmly opened it, picking at the tape. Hannah rolled her eyes and mimed looking at her watch. When he opened the little box underneath all the paper, he stopped for a moment, dangling a long silver chain in the light of the moon.

"Well, this is beautiful," he said, astonished.

Hannah turned it to show him their initials carved together in the silver. "I don't know if you wear necklaces, but I wanted you to have it."

"I'll wear it, don't you worry." He put it on, and Hannah helped him with the clasp. She felt his hands trembling and was surprised.

"Emily," Matthew began, wincing at the name, "she never gave me anything. Not even for my birthday."

Hannah waited for him to feel sad, but instead he looked up, his face happy and relaxed.

"Thank you," he said, wrapping his arms around her in a giant hug.

The next day, Hannah was pleased to see the silver chain under Matthew's shirt collar. The light reflected off it, catching the silver. It made her feel she had some sort of claim on him, some sort of mark. She wondered if he felt that way about the leaf and pearl necklace that she wore.

That night at the Otter, Lily teased them mercilessly upon seeing Matthew's necklace, saying they would soon start dressing alike. Hannah teased her back, saying Mr. Rich probably had a ring just like hers on his hand.

June came quickly, and then it was the day when her family was due to arrive. Hannah had everything set. She had e-mailed her mom with instructions to get onto the coach from the airport, and with the address of the bed and breakfast she had reserved for them. The B&B was a really cute one near the river. She knew they would like to walk along the river first thing in the morning. Hannah hoped she would be able to wake up early enough to join them.

Hannah and Matthew waited in a nearby coffeehouse, eating *pain au chocolat* and drinking cappuccino. Her aunt had just called them from the B&B to say they had arrived, and they all wanted to take showers. Matthew and Hannah agreed to meet them at their hotel in an hour. Matthew could not stop looking at his watch as they finished their coffee.

"Relax." Hannah patted his hand, laughing. "We have a whole hour!"

They decided to walk along the river near the B&B, as they still had time before meeting Hannah's family. Weeping willows leaned over the water, and swans gracefully glided down the still river. Hannah thought it looked like a painting. The summer air was warm, and the light reflected softly off the water.

Looking up at Matthew, she commented, "You're wearing your favorite shirt today."

"Yes, just to look ... you know, respectable," Matthew admitted. The shirt was a dark teal color that brought out the color of his eyes. It had a collar and looked as if it was silk. It was neatly ironed.

"You look very respectable! More than usual," Hannah said, hitting him jokingly with a map to the B&B she had printed out.

"Do you think they will like me?" Matthew asked nervously.

"Why wouldn't they?" Hannah asked, surprised. He had real concern in his eyes.

"Well ... I'm probably not the sort of bloke they imagined for you. I am into sports, you know. I'm just good at polo. You and Lil, you two could find doctors, lawyers ... real brains to be with."

"Matthew, I can't believe you feel that way! I didn't realize ..." Hannah chewed her lip, trying to remember whether she had ever mentioned liking a medical student or law student. She couldn't think of any reason Matthew would feel she wanted more of a "brain."

"Anyway," said to him, "you are a brain! You got better grades than me last term!"

"Well, in sports medicine and therapy!" Matthew replied. "That is not exactly statistics and population genetics—whatever that is!"

"Look ..." Hannah tried to explain, stopping to look up at him. "That stuff may be easy for you, but I am so uncoordinated. I would never be good at sports. I admire you for that. And I'm sure if you had the same classes I do, you'd do great at them."

Matthew did not looked convinced. He was looking down at a swan in the river, not at Hannah.

"You're good at what you do. You have talent. And I would love you even if you weren't smart and talented. Which you are." Hannah cupped his chin with her hand and turned his face to hers.

"Okay?" she asked.

Matthew smiled and then took a deep breath. "Okay. Let's meet them," he said, taking Hannah's hand.

"Did … did Emily's parents not … like you?" Hannah asked hesitantly, once they resumed walking.

"Never met them," he replied, his face stony.

"Well … I can already tell you mine are crazy about you. I've shown them your pictures and told them loads of stories. They practically know you. You don't have to worry," Hannah explained, watching his face.

Matthew nodded.

When they reached the B&B, they found Hannah's mother and father wandering nearby, gazing into the river.

"Hannah!" her mother shrieked upon seeing Hannah and Matthew. She flung her arms around Hannah. "And you must be Matthew," her mom said, smiling. She held her hand out.

"Thank you ever so much for the cup. It was a sweet thought," Matthew said somewhat woodenly. Hannah wondered if he had practiced saying it in his head.

"Well, Hannah, you didn't tell me he was a gentleman, too!" Her mom grinned at Hannah.

Hannah's dad also shook Matthew's hand, and they exchanged somewhat stiff, formal greetings. Hannah began to feel tense.

"So, how was the flight?" she asked, hanging onto Matthew's hand, which was sweating.

"Oh, you know," her mom rolled her eyes. "Long. But it's so lovely here! Even more beautiful than I hoped!" she pointed to the river.

"Hannah! Matthew!" a voice rang out. Hannah looked up at the B&B to see that her aunt had appeared at the door. Her gray hair, normally shoulder length, had grown much longer, and was streaming out behind her. She leaped down the stairs to the river below and enveloped Hannah in a hug. Hannah noticed that her aunt had the bag from Tibet that she had given her for Christmas over her shoulder. Matthew held his hand out for a handshake, but Laura threw her arms around his shoulders and pressed against him. Matthew hugged her, looking at Hannah in surprise.

"My. A strong one!" Aunt Laura felt his shoulders and arms. "Well, Hannah's lucky, isn't she!"

Hannah felt herself blushing, but Matthew laughed. "It's great to meet the Hannahs. I've been waiting for this for a long time!" he beamed.

Hannah felt herself relax. Matthew was joking around again, back to his normal self.

"So, you play polo?" Laura took Matthew's arm as they all began walking toward the city's center. "Is it frightening, to be on a horse?"

For the next ten minutes or so, Matthew entertained Laura with stories of polo accidents. Hannah kept her attention partly on their conversation, hearing Laura's gasp when Matthew told her about the time his horse reared up and he was thrown onto his back. Hannah walked slightly ahead with her parents, pointing out the trees and flowers growing by the river.

When they reached King's College, her mother gazed

at it, open-mouthed.

"It's so big! Much bigger than I imagined from your pictures!" she said. Her father got out his camera, and they took ten pictures of the college at different angles in the first few minutes. Then, they took ten more of Hannah, Matthew, and the family by the college from different angles. When Matthew proposed getting a coffee at King's bar, a look of shock crossed her aunt's face.

"We can have coffee in there?" she asked, amazed.

"I go there all the time for coffee now," Hannah told her family.

Her parents and her aunt returned to the B&B to rest for a few hours after the coffee in King's College. That evening, Matthew, Hannah, and Lily met them at the White Otter pub. Hannah was relieved to see Matthew and her mother speaking to each other, even if it was only about the menu.

"What's bangers and mash?" her mom asked, pronouncing the words slowly.

"Sausage with mashed potatoes," Matthew explained. Her mother decided to order it. Hannah's parents then asked Matthew which beers to try, and Matthew brought out his list. They combed through it, discussing the various subtle differences of the various beers in color and taste. As her parents discussed the beers with Matthew, Aunt Laura studied the otter pictures on the walls with a wistful smile. Hannah leaned over to Lily to relate to her how tense Matthew had been about meeting her parents. Lily looked at her with understanding eyes.

"Well you know, it can break a relationship if the mum or dad doesn't approve," Lily explained.

"I know, but they already knew so much about

Matthew, and anyway, I wouldn't have broken up with him even if they didn't all get along!" Hannah replied.

Lily nodded. "Still. Now he can relax. They haven't run screaming." Lily joked, and Hannah punched her arm playfully.

Her aunt watched them, smiling. But then she leaned over to Hannah.

"I don't want to worry you," she said in a low whisper, "but I think Mr. Wrong heard us discussing our trip out here, at the mall."

Hannah's suddenly found it hard to breathe. She clenched the table edge with both hands. "Wh… what?"

"We were talking, your mom and I, about how happy you seem out here. Near Nine West, you know, by the fountain?"

Hannah nodded.

"I said how excited I was about coming to Cambridge. I turned a little bit, because I thought a man was listening closely to us, and it looked like … well, I couldn't be sure. It looked like the man, the boy, who came to the house looking for you. It seemed like he had heard us."

Hannah smiled weakly. "Well," she considered. "He's far away. Maybe he will just leave me alone. Maybe he didn't hear."

Her aunt nodded. "I'm sure you're right, dear. I'm sure it was just my imagination."

A small twist in Hannah's stomach made it difficult for her to eat the fish and chips when it came. But she told herself Bret probably hadn't been in the mall, and that her aunt was just needlessly worrying. Besides, he wouldn't come all this way to find her, right? she asked herself.

The name *Bret* was not mentioned for the remainder of the week. Matthew grew more relaxed every day, and joked incessantly with Aunt Laura, telling her the most shocking stories he could think of. At the end of their visit, her dad had tried most of the beers on Matthew's list. Hannah's mother was the only one who hadn't bonded particularly with Matthew, but Hannah thought that she liked him. Her mother shook his hand when they parted, and told him to take care of Hannah. Her parents and her aunt returned home with suitcases full of tea and King's College memorabilia. They promised to return soon.

Chapter 14 – The White Otter

A few weeks later, Matthew, Hannah, and Lily sat around a small wooden table at the White Otter pub. They were celebrating their freedom from classes and the warm summer weather. For Hannah, it wasn't warm enough to be mid-July, but she agreed that the long days made up for it. Hannah and Lily were doing their master's research in the library much of the time, but as the evenings were light until ten, they had plenty of daylight hours to enjoy Cambridge.

Lily looked outside at the light sky and gushed about how lovely Cambridge was in the summer.

"The light is just a perfect golden color," she said, and Hannah nodded in agreement.

"I can't believe it's nine!" Hannah exclaimed. "It looks like afternoon."

"More time to toast and drink!" Lily cheerfully raised her glass. She toasted to her last term of college housing. As of one week before, she was officially living with Tom. She had stopped calling him "Mr. Rich" but still flashed her ruby ring whenever she mentioned him.

Matthew excused himself to go to the bathroom. He had been strangely quiet all evening, and Hannah kept catching him staring at the otter sketch just above Lily's head. Hannah watched him go, concerned. But then she leaned in to Lily.

"I've been wanting to ask you. So, you and Tom are living together … does it mean you are engaged?" she asked in a hushed, excited tone.

"Well," Lily blushed. "I'm not sure when he'll ask, but I think he is going to do it soon. After all, he knows my ring size already." She laughed. "And he has made comments and questions about wedding venues … you know, where I could see myself getting married … one day. I think living together is …"

"A good first step," a low voice near her ear spoke. Hannah jumped, and then looked up to see Matthew climbing into the seat next to her.

"You made me jump!" Hannah hit him with a napkin. Then she kissed his cheek.

"I forgive you," Hannah smiled at Matthew and grabbed his arm. "I'll get you back."

"I'm sure you will," Matthew laughed. Hannah sometimes hid in the bathroom, or under the bed, ready to leap out at Matthew when he least suspected it.

"You've been quiet tonight. Are you all right?" Hannah asked.

Matthew's smile faded. "Yes, but … well, I do have something to talk to you about. But I'll ask you later, okay?" he looked over at Lily, who was watching them.

Hannah nodded, but her eyebrows furrowed, and she frowned, wondering what it could be.

"Well, there is something I'll ask you now …" Matthew looked at Hannah, thinking. "I have noticed you have been jumpy lately. Ever since …"

" … your family came," Lily finished. "Yeah, I noticed that, too. You have seemed so tense in the last weeks. Did we say something your … your parents didn't like?" Lily asked with wide eyes.

"No! No!" Hannah grabbed at Lily's hand and Matthew's arm. "Oh, they loved you both! Totally!" She looked at Matthew. "All three of them liked you guys."

Matthew let out a breath of air. "Phew … though I did feel like it went well, I sort of noticed you're a bit … I don't know, so I worried something … didn't go well."

Hannah studied her glass, still half-full of cider. "Well … I hate to bring up the guy, this Bret guy, again. But … my aunt thinks he heard them talking about coming to Cambridge to visit me …" Hannah explained.

Two voices spoke at once.

"He knows you're here?" Matthew asked, alarmed.

"What … that bloke? Didn't he run off with his ex-fiancée"?" Lily asked, confused.

Hannah proceeded to tell Lily the whole story of how he snuck into her room in San Francisco during Christmas and demanded they get back together. Matthew stiffened when Hannah explained how he snuck through her window, and she massaged his shoulders to try to relax him as she told the story.

"The vamp … I mean the … nasty woman dumped him," Hannah explained to Lily.

"Anyway, I got away," Hannah gave Matthew a reassuring pat. "And I don't think he knows where I am … unless he … knows where I am." Hannah now hid her head in her hands for a moment. "I'm overreacting, right?"

"I'm sure he wouldn't blow a ticket to come all this

way, when he's obviously not wanted," Matthew patted her hand. "I mean, Emily would never do something like that. They seem alike. Want you when you're around, forget about you when you're not there. I don't know the bloke, but I don't see him going to the effort to come all this way."

Hannah nodded.

"Besides," Matthew continued, "that was probably your aunt's fear speaking. She probably didn't really see him in the mall—it was most likely some other bloke."

Hannah nodded again.

"Why didn't you tell me before?" Lily asked. "This is news to me ... six months later?"

Hannah reached for her hand. "Oh, I knew it, I knew you'd be mad, but I just wanted to leave it behind me. I didn't ... want anyone to know, but Matthew called on the very day after it happened and could tell I was shaken up."

"Matthew called you on Christmas?" Lily smiled meaningfully. "That's nice, Mattie."

Matthew actually blushed. "You better have told me, even if I hadn't called. I have to know these things, what happens to you," he said to Hannah. She nodded.

Lily twined her hair around her finger as she stared at the table. Finally she exclaimed, "That vamp!"

Hannah paled.

"I mean, what a witch!" Lily continued. "To steal him from you, then dump him again like nothing happened? What is it with women!"

Hannah stared, surprised.

"Anyway, you are better off without him. I mean, look what a good thing you have now." Lily motioned to Matthew, and Hannah smiled. "A witch like that will probably come back again and again, just to rob him of whatever happiness he finds, torment him, chew him up, and spit him out. He will probably see her in another year, just when he's back on his feet."

Hannah laughed drily. "Yeah, but it usually takes her a century to revisit ..." she joked, then bit her lip as Matthew stared at her with a strange expression.

"But you know," Hannah continued, "it wasn't all her. I mean, he went with her. He ignored me completely and let her ..."

" ... do that, I know," Lily pointed to the scars on her neck. "When Bret says he was trying to protect you by dumping you, I can believe him when I see what she did to you."

"Yeah," Hannah admitted. "He did say he never stopped loving me, that he was trying to protect me by ... by ... ignoring me."

Matthew stared at Hannah's neck with a curious expression.

"Wait, wait," Matthew interjected. "I thought Bret did that to your neck." He ran his fingers over the tiny marks.

"Well," Hannah admitted, cursing herself for having lied to Lily about Tressie causing the scars. "He actually did. But it was the only time he ... I mean, hurt me, and he wasn't trying to hurt me, really."

"Pfft!" Matthew made a sound and threw up his hands. "They always say that. Why are you protecting him? You know what? He did mean to hurt you. Emily meant to hurt me. These are cruel, violent people. And if I ever see him I'll ..." Matthew mimed a fist punching his face and turned red.

"No!" Hannah cried. She covered his fist with her hand. "Promise to stay away from him!" Her voice was almost hysterical. "I don't want you hurt over me!"

"I can hold my own in a fight, you know," Matthew argued.

Hannah shook her head sadly, and Matthew continued.

"What! I'm fit, all that polo. I used to do rugby, you know! What, is he a black belt or something?

"He's … a monster," Hannah whispered in a hushed tone.

Matthew looked uncomfortable, and Lily stepped back into the conversation.

"Wait … I'm sure you told me that *she* did that to your neck," she said, pointing at the scars. "I thought this Bret was relatively okay. Spineless, but nice."

Hannah sighed. "There are two scars," she invented. "One from him, one from her. And … he isn't nice. He's not like your first-year love, who took you on picnics."

A sad look passed over Lily's face when Hannah brought up Amos, her first-year boyfriend.

"He has no morals," Hannah continued. "That's why he's so dangerous to you, Matthew. You would never hurt someone … not unless you had to. And you would st … stop."

Matthew looked alarmed.

"I just … I just don't know what to do … if he comes here," Hannah lamented, covering her face again.

"Listen, Hannah, he can't be that bad. You loved him, right? So, he had to have some good in him," Lily commented. Matthew stiffened at the word *love*. Hannah entwined her fingers around Matthew's.

"No," she said meaningfully, looking into Matthew's eyes. "I really did think I loved him. But now I know what love is." She turned to Lily. "I wasn't in love with Bret. I was more … charmed. Enchanted." She leaned her head against Matthew's shoulder.

"Well," Lily stood up to go to the bathroom. "Sounds like a fairytale. Like a dark fairytale."

Hannah remembered Lily's story of the picnics by the river with Amos. "Your story does, too. But a nicer one."

"Well," Lily flashed her ring. "I prefer the real thing."

"Me, too," Hannah said honestly. She looked up at Matthew with a warm feeling flushing her cheeks. "Me, too."

But he was not looking at her eyes. He was scanning the scars on her neck, tracing the two tiny marks with his finger.

"I think it's time to go," Hannah stood up, but Lily motioned for her to sit back down.

"No, no, the night is young, and I have some news to tell. Let's end on a better note! I'll get more cider when I come back from the loo." Lily motioned to the empty glasses.

"I'll get the drinks," Matthew offered and went to the bar. Hannah sat at the table, staring out at the still-light sky. She felt silly for worrying; of course Bret would not come all this way. Hannah had made it clear she was not interested. Her aunt was probably just imagining that he was there in the mall, anyway.

Her breath came easier. She realized she had not been

breathing well when Bret came into the conversation. But she was safe, she reminded herself. She took a deep breath. She wished she had told Matthew and Lily about this earlier. She felt better just talking about it.

Matthew returned with two ciders and a lager for himself. Seeing him balancing three glasses in his hands, Hannah gasped. "Oh! I should have helped you carry them!"

"It's all right, love," he mussed her hair. "You looked distracted—I saw you from the bar. What were you thinking about? Him again?"

Hannah shook her head. "No. Not really. I was thinking how glad I am that I told you and Lil the whole story. You're right, he won't come all this way." She smiled.

"Tell me everything. Always," he said and kissed her forehead.

Then he paused. He opened his mouth to say something, but at that moment, Lily swooped back to the table. She grabbed her cider, thanked Matthew, and then leaned in to them both, eyes wide. "So," Lily began. "We were discussing Amos, Mr. Fairytale, right?"

Hannah nodded.

"Well, just this morning, he rang me."

"What?" Hannah asked.

"Wait," Matthew interrupted. "Who is this guy, the someone you dated in your first year?"

Lily gave him the short version of the story, about how they dated for one year, and then he broke it off to get engaged to "Mummy's choice," as she put it.

"Well, here we are, four years later and it ended. Just days before the wedding!" Lily exclaimed.

"He left her?" Hannah asked, shocked.

"No! She left him! Poor bloke. I feel sorry for him. The little princess met someone else. Amos is heartbroken. Cried on the phone like I was his mum! Of course his mum had it coming, for making him break up with me. Can you imagine the embarrassment ... the wedding canceled only days before the date!" Lily smiled evilly.

"My gosh!" Hannah asked, her eyes wide. "What will you do?"

"Well, nothing, really. I'm with Tom now, aren't I?" Lily wiggled her fingers. "I'm not giving him up. I told Amos it's over between us. I've moved on."

Lily took a long drink of cider as Hannah shook her head. "Oh Lily, I'm sorry. It must be confusing."

"No, not for me," Lily said adamantly, shaking her brown curls. "Maybe for Amos. But I know what I want. Tom. Besides, I could never trust Amos the same way I trusted him before."

Hannah nodded and patted Lily's hand. Lily turned to Matthew.

"So," Lily said," Hannah has told us her dark tale. I've shared my news. Is there anything you would like to share with us?" She raised her eyebrows at Matthew.

"He doesn't like to talk about Emily," Hannah explained as he stared into his beer.

"Well," Matthew looked up. "Not much to say. Selfish girl. Wanted to be with a 'polo boy,' she used to say. It's over. End of story."

Lily surprised Hannah by leaning into the table toward him. "Isn't there ... something else?" she asked in a low voice, moving her eyebrows up and down comically.

Matthew stared into his beer again, and drummed

his fingers on the table. "What is it?" Hannah asked, turning to him.

"Okay. I wanted to ask you … well, you know how Mr. R … Tom and Lily are living together now?"

Hannah nodded.

"Well, don't you think it's a good idea?" Matthew asked.

"Yes, it's great!" Hannah nodded enthusiastically. She patted Lily's hand.

Lily rolled her eyes. "Just *ask* her," she said in an exhausted tone.

Matthew cleared his throat. "I'm trying to say … girlfriend, boyfriend … doesn't it make sense to live together?" Hannah's eyes were now as round as her mouth.

"Are you asking me to move in with you?" Hannah asked. Matthew nodded and gulped nervously.

"You could save on rent!" Lily pitched in.

Hannah giggled. "It's a great idea," she told Matthew, whose face filled with relief. "And not just because of the rent."

Then Hannah gasped. "No communal kitchen!" she realized.

"Well, there would be a communal kitchen … shared by you and me." He grinned.

"Would there be Wheatabix in the kitchen?" Hannah mocked Matthew's breakfast cereal. "Because then I'm not sure about this living together thing …"

They laughed, and then Hannah bit her lip. "But how will I tell my parents this? They'll freak."

"I think maybe we could tell your aunt first, and she can break the news to your parents. She seemed open-minded." Matthew suggested.

"Wow! Great idea. You have been thinking about this, haven't you?" Hannah asked.

Matthew nodded with a grin. "I actually think your dad will like the idea. He told me to protect you, when he left for the States."

"Okay, I'll call Aunt Laura tomorrow." Hannah paused. "I'm so excited!" She burst into a sudden grin and flung her arms around Matthew.

Lily stamped her feet with an excited smile. "Move to north Cambridge, near Tom and me! We can have dinner parties at each other's houses!"

"Maybe I should call my aunt tonight," Hannah reasoned. "It's afternoon in California."

"Good idea, we'll ring her when we get to my room. And by the way, it's 'ring.'" Matthew teased.

"No way," Hannah replied. "If there's going to be Wheatabix in the kitchen, I get to keep saying 'call.'"

Matthew sighed and put his head in his hands. "Obviously we have loads of issues to work through."

Hannah giggled. They decided to head home for the evening, so Hannah could phone her aunt before it got too late. Lily waved excitedly when they parted ways, and Matthew looked happy and relieved on the way back. Hannah, however, chewed her lip as she walked the streets of Cambridge, now dark. Holding Matthew's hand, she felt safe. But thinking of her dad's words to Matthew sent a chill up her back. Matthew couldn't protect her. Not against Bret.

Chapter 15 – Moving In

The July days passed into August. Hannah and Lily had made progress with their research, and Matthew was tan and fit from all the polo. Lily and Tom seemed happy living together, and Matthew and Hannah had already found a place to move into in September. Lily had even met Amos for coffee a few times to help him get back on his feet.

On the last weekend of August, Matthew was speaking on the phone to his sister "up north." Hannah lay on her bed in her room, flipping through a National Geographic magazine.

"Elisa's pregnant!" Matthew mouthed to Hannah, and she mimed clapping. She rolled over and saw a newspaper sticking out of Matthew's backpack. She pointed to it.

"Can I read this?" she mouthed. He nodded, and she pulled the paper out. A book fell to the floor with a thump. Hannah stared at the title, feeling faint.

"Vampyre Stories," she read. She looked up at Matthew questioningly, and he held up a finger, asking her to wait.

"Um, can I call you later? Give my love to everyone there," Matthew finished the conversation and hung up the phone.

"Hannah," he said gently, and hearing her name snapped her out of her silence.

"Why, but … why do you even *have* this? Did … you didn't sss … see anything strange …" she stuttered. "I mean, you don't even like science fiction."

"Look," Matthew came closer to where Hannah was seated on the bed. "I know it sounds crazy. But … I've been wondering …"

Hannah's heart skipped as he traced a finger along the scars on her neck.

"These look like teeth marks. As if someone bit you. Am I right?" Matthew asked hesitantly.

Hannah said nothing. Then she nodded.

"I knew it!" Matthew said, relief in his voice. "It all makes sense now! Why you lied to Lily about who gave you the scars. You're ashamed. But Hannah," he lifted her chin with his finger. "You don't have to be. We've all done things we regret. It's called living."

Hannah's eyes narrowed in thought, her heart beating rapidly. "Ashamed?" she asked herself. Then she remembered, as if he was there, Bret's cool mouth on hers, those seductive lips. She remembered thinking, those lips have killed, as she kissed him. His eyes were so deep, so old, staring into hers.

"Yes. I am ashamed, you're right," Hannah admitted. Girls had gone missing because of Bret. She had nearly been one of them.

"The words you use. *Charmed, enchanted. Monster!*" Matthew half-whispered in a hushed, excited voice. "I've been wanting so long to ask you, but I was afraid to upset you. This bloke … he likes to … dress as a vampire, right?"

"Dress ... dress as a ..." Hannah said, confused.

"Fangs and all! I read about them," Matthew motioned to the book. "Know thine enemy. They actually believe they are vampires. They stay out of the sun. Avoid foods with garlic. Wear plastic fangs."

"Um ... he thought he was a vampire, yeah," Hannah said, not really lying.

"I've been reading up," Matthew admitted. "In case that bloke comes here, shows his face, or his fangs." Matthew laughed, but Hannah did not. He suddenly sobered and held her.

"Oh Han, it's all right. We've all done crazy things. It's life. We make mistakes." Matthew soothed.

"You don't think ... I'm tainted?" Hannah asked.

"No! You don't dress up in black clothes and wear fangs, do you?"

Hannah shook her head.

"Look, Emily was every bit the monster he is. Every inch," Matthew told her, and touched her scar. "But to go that far, to break skin. How could he?"

"I wanted it," Hannah admitted. "I believed ..."

"What, that he was a vampire?" Matthew laughed again.

Hannah said in a whisper, "That biting me was the right thing..." Then she stood up. "Okay," she continued, "Now you know. But you don't need to read those books. He's not coming here. I'm not going back to San Francisco."

Matthew pulled Hannah to him. "Okay. But it was just to understand it all more clearly. And Hannah ..."

Hannah met his clear, honest blue eyes.

"You could have told me. I don't like secrets. I'm glad I know," he explained.

Hannah smiled weakly. "I'm glad you know, too. At least part of it."

Matthew's forehead creased. "Will you tell me the rest? You didn't date someone who dresses as a werewolf, did you?"

Hannah laughed. "No, but … there is more about Bret, but I don't want to talk about it. I want this in the past."

"The past is part of us," Matthew responded.

"True," Hannah admitted.

"Will you tell it all to me, one day?" Matthew asked, tracing Hannah's lips with this finger.

Hannah thought for a moment. "Maybe," she replied.

"Okay," Matthew smiled. "That's good enough for now."

Hannah curled up in Matthew's arms. She felt relieved that he was closer to knowing the truth about Bret. She felt more connected to him. And she felt like he was in on the secret, in a way. But what if she did tell him Bret was actually a vampire? Would Matthew run away from her, assuming she was crazy? Hannah closed her eyes and tried not to think about it.

Chapter 16 – The Secret

September arrived. Within a week, summer was over. It began to rain, and a chilly wind blew through Cambridge. Hannah thought back to the fall just one year ago, when she had felt constantly cold. This fall, she felt constantly warm. She knew it was because of Matthew. Whenever she thought about moving in with him, she felt a hot glow run through her.

Two days later, Hannah stood outside the Cambridge bus station, waiting for the coach from Heathrow to deliver her aunt. Her aunt had agreed to help move Hannah and Matthew and then report back to Hannah's parents on the safeness of the new location.

Her aunt stepped off the bus. Her long, gray hair streamed out behind her. She was in her "traveling clothes," which consisted of long, loose, flowing pants and an oversized sweatshirt. Hannah couldn't help thinking how Californian she looked, with her long hair, tan face, and bead necklace. Her aunt was scanning the people waiting around them, and finally met eyes with Hannah. Her aunt broke out into a happy smile.

"Hannah bug!" she screamed. They moved toward each other and then wrapped their arms around each other in a hug. Then Aunt Laura held Hannah at arm's length.

"You look so happy! Oh, I'm so excited you're moving in with him. You're not engaged, are you, dear?"

Laura studied Hannah's hands, finding no ring.

"No, not yet …" Hannah blushed.

"Well, I didn't think so. I told your parents that of course you would have told us if you had gotten engaged!" her aunt remarked.

"So mom … she's really okay with this? I mean, us living together even though were not … engaged, even?" Hannah asked, as the coach driver unloaded the bags.

"Well," her aunt sighed. "You know your mom, of course at first she thought it was too soon, and you're not married, and all of that. But your dad was thrilled. He kept pointing out how you would be safer living with a man, and of course Matthew's such an angel. Your mom loves him. She'll come around in the end."

The porter unloaded her aunt's bag, and Hannah moved to grab it. At that point, she locked eyes with a boy coming out of the coach. A flash of green met her eyes, and as his gaze found hers, she felt dizzy.

He looked triumphant. Hannah thought irrationally, "Why did the day have to be overcast. Why couldn't it be sunny?" Only moments later, the fear came.

She gave Bret the coldest, stoniest face she thought possible, and his triumphant smile turned confused. Then she seized her aunt's arm and turned to leave.

"Let's go," Hannah said, taking her aunt's bag. "It looks like rain."

Her aunt looked nervously at the sky. Hannah's college housing was close enough to the bus station to walk. However, Hannah was nervous Bret would follow them there.

"Aunt Laura, let's take a taxi," Hannah improvised. "Wouldn't you like to take a quick tour of Cambridge before we go home?"

"But dear, isn't your room very near here?" Aunt Laura asked, looking confused.

"It really looks like rain, I think it's going to be a bad storm," Hannah invented as she began to climb into a taxi. "I really think we'd be better off in a car for now."

Hannah gave the driver directions to drive around the city, and to drop them off at the side entrance to her housing, which was on a narrow alley. She then nervously watched out the window, but Bret did not seem to be following them either on foot or by taxi. When they reached her building, she quickly grabbed her aunt's bags and ushered her through the front door. Hannah slammed the door closed as soon as they got to her room.

"Oh dear, I'm quite tired from the journey. Do you mind if I take a shower to refresh myself? Then I'd love to go out for fish and chips!" Laura said.

Hannah nodded to her aunt and retrieved a towel from her chest of drawers. Her aunt unzipped her large blue suitcase and took out a yellow-and-blue-striped vanity case, then disappeared down the hall to the communal shower. And, without turning, Hannah suddenly knew that he was there.

"What," Hannah said firmly. "What do you want?"

"You," the melodic voice whispered into her ear, at her neck. She moved away. "Come home with me," he pleaded.

"No. My life is here," Hannah said, not wanting to

turn around, to see his face.

"Your short life. Your mortal life." His voice was cruel. He put his hands on her shoulders and turned her to him.

"I am offering you more," Bret whispered as he met her gaze. She was dizzy … falling … then she blinked. She twisted away from him.

"I've moved on. So have you. When Tressie showed up, you moved on big-time. Well, it's over between us. Forever." Hannah pointed at her window.

"No, I haven't moved on." Bret came up to Hannah and held her shoulders in a firm grasp. "I'm still in love with you. You're my only love," he traced the scars on her neck with a smooth, chilly finger. "Let's finish where we left off," he murmured in a low, melodic tone.

"No!" Hannah said firmly, shaking her head to clear it. She felt dizzy with him so close. "Can't you see I don't love you? Not anymore. Not ever!"

Bret's eyes grew sharp. "Come with me now," he demanded. Hannah shook her head no.

Bret sighed. "You force my hand. I can smell your aunt, you know. All the way down the hallway." He sneered and pointed to the picture of Matthew, framed by her bedside. "I can find him, too. Your human morsel … your fling …"

"I love him!" Hannah screamed. "I love my aunt, too, and I don't want her to be frightened. If you love me, you'll leave. Leave me alone."

Hannah gasped as Bret's eyes flashed with rage. "That's not love," he growled, pointing at the picture of Matthew. "That's comfort! You loved me once. You can again." Then he grabbed her and kissed her. Hannah's heart stopped beating, then beat erratically. She felt dizzy. She felt sick. It was nothing like before. The dizziness had always been a comfort, or even exciting, like flying. Now it felt alien. She didn't like it.

Bret's face looked expectant. Then he frowned as he studied Hannah's face. His eyes grew small and looked mean. "You better come. Because if you don't …"—Bret pointed to Matthew's picture—" … *his* life won't go on much longer." Bret smiled then, and it was the smile of a fiend; all his teeth showed.

"Think about it," he smiled again and disappeared out the window.

A second later, the door opened, and a much cleaner version of Hannah's aunt entered. "What's wrong?" she asked immediately, setting her toiletry bag down. "Did something happen?"

Hannah shook her head. "N … nothing," she said unconvincingly.

"You're white as a ghost! And your lip is bleeding. Did you bite it?"

Hannah wiped her hand across her mouth and saw a smear of red.

"Oh yeah … it's just that … a noise startled me," she invented.

"Well, let's go, then, to that pub we went to this summer. The Swimming Otter or something like that. I would love some fish and chips. Is Matthew coming? Oh! I almost forgot!" Her aunt turned to rummage in her suitcase. "These are from your mom," she held up some patterned kitchen towels. "For the new place."

Hannah's eyes welled up with tears. "What's wrong, dear?" her aunt asked again.

"Oh," Hannah said, and her voice shook. "I'm just … thinking of home, and missing it."

Her aunt hugged her. "Give Matthew a call. You'll feel better when you talk to him."

"Okay," Hannah said. She pulled out her cell phone. "Come to the Otter for fish and chips with my aunt," she texted.

She read his message a second later. "Okay, he's coming to the pub," Hannah said. She took a long look at the kitchen towels. "Tell mom thanks … it means … a lot," Hannah whispered.

"Well, you can tell her yourself, dear! Let's call her tomorrow."

"Tomorrow …" Hannah whispered, and hid her face in her hair. They left for the pub, Hannah thankful for the dark night so her aunt could not see her terrified expression.

Chapter 17 – The Otter

As soon as they walked into the Otter, Matthew waved from a small table in the far corner. Relief washed over Hannah's face when she saw him, smiling and safe.

"What's wrong?" he asked immediately, when they sat down.

"Homesick," her aunt explained after greeting Matthew with a hug. "I showed her the kitchen towels from her mom. She wanted to give you both a gift for the new place." Laura patted Matthew on the knee.

Matthew muttered a thank-you, still looking at Hannah's face with alarm. "Shall Hannah and I get some drinks?" he asked Laura. "While you look over the menu?"

"Oh, I know what I want! Fish and chips! I'll get the drinks. It will be fun. I like using English pounds. It's like a game!" Laura exclaimed as she got up to go to the bar. Hannah and Matthew asked her to order fish and chips for them as well, along with a cider and beer. As soon as Aunt Laura left for the bar, Matthew slid in closer to Hannah.

"So … what's really wrong?" he asked.

"Bret's … here," Hannah said in a shocked voice. She

proceeded to tell Matthew the whole story.

"But you told him to sod off. You don't think he'll listen? Maybe he gets it now, maybe he'll go home."

Hannah shook her head.

"He threatened you. And Aunt Laura," she explained.

"I'm not leaving you alone, then. In fact, I hope he shows his face. I'd like to introduce my fist to it."

"Matthew, you have to promise to stay out of it. He's dangerous."

"Oh, and I'm not?"

"Look, he has no morals. He could really hurt us all."

"So we'll go to the police," Matthew suggested.

"And tell them what? That he broke into my room?"

"For starters, yes."

"He's not afraid of the police. He can disappear. And take me with him."

Hannah shuddered. Matthew put his arm protectively around her.

"I won't let you disappear," he promised.

Hannah snuggled up to him and felt safer. A tiny voice in her mind, though, told her the safe feeling was just an illusion.

As Aunt Laura passed the window on her way back to the table, she saw a face and waved happily. Hannah turned to see Lily, a wide grin on her face. Lily bounded into the pub and broke the sober atmosphere.

"Look, you lot!" she beamed. "I'm engaged!" Lily held out her hand, and a giant diamond flashed. Hannah forgot her worries for a moment.

"Wow," all three said, taking turns examining the

ring. "Isn't it exciting? Tom just proposed today! I was hoping you'd be at the Otter," Lily exclaimed, her cheeks red.

They invited her to join them for fish and chips, and Lily went to the bar to order. Hannah went to the bar with her to order another drink, since she had nervously drained her cider already. Suddenly a hand was around her wrist, restraining her. The hand was cool and strong. It did not feel at all like Matthew's normally warm hand. It closed more tightly around Hannah's wrist, and, because she was afraid to look up, she stared at the bar in front of her.

"So," a low voice whispered in her ear. "Are you coming?"

Hannah looked wordlessly up at Bret as he tightened his grip. Lily looked confused. "Hannah?" she asked. "Who is this?"

Hannah tried to pull herself out of Bret's iron grip. Then everything happened in slow motion.

Her aunt saw them and dropped her napkin. Matthew stood up, furious, and started to run toward them. Lily took a step closer to Bret and then froze, horror on her face.

Hannah wiggled like a fish, she thought, her arm caught in Bret's grasp.

Three large men approached and formed a semicircle around Hannah and Bret. Hannah breathed with relief when she saw that Matthew could not get past them. Matthew's furious eyes were on Bret.

"Unhand this girl," one deep voice said.

"Are you having trouble, lass?" a kindly voice asked her.

"I'm calling the police, unless you let go of her," an angrier voice spoke.

The men moved in. To Hannah's surprise, Bret let go of her arm. "Later," he whispered into her ear. His mouth curved into a smile, and then he was gone.

Matthew and the other men looked around, confused. "Here one moment, the next gone," a voice said.

"Where did he get off to?" another voice spoke.

"Must be ill, didn't look at all well," Hannah heard.

A hand gently grabbed Hannah's shoulder. She felt herself being steadied. "All right, lass?" the kind voice asked, and she nodded. Then she looked up to see Matthew coming toward her, and she fell into his arms.

Her aunt was close behind. "I'm so sorry!" she spluttered, red-faced. "He must have followed me all the way … on the plane, the bus! I feel awful!"

"No," Hannah said, her voice shaking. "He would have found me anyway, eventually."

Lily grabbed Hannah's arm, her brown eyes wide and fierce. "Hannah, what's wrong with him?"

"I don't know … I don't know why he won't just let me go," Hannah answered.

"No. What's. Wrong. With. Him. I saw his face. I saw hi …" Lily's voice shook.

Hannah stared at her friend. Did she know?

"There's something … something not right …" Lily was angry, and her fingernails dug into Hannah's arm. Hannah winced.

"Give her a rest," Matthew untangled Lily's fingers from Hannah's arm. "She's going to faint."

"Let's get her to a table." Aunt Laura suggested.

Aunt Laura and Matthew helped Hannah to the

table. She sat down, shaking. The bartender brought over a scotch, and she drank it quickly.

"I have to go …" Lily said, flustered. "I need some air." She grabbed her bag and had left the pub before Aunt Laura could finish saying, "No, stay …"

Four steaming plates of fish and chips arrived at the table. Hannah was shaking. "What will I do? He'll find me as soon as I'm alone."

"Look." Matthew was still red-faced with anger. "I'll talk to him. He cannot terrorize you like this. He's not wanted. I'll explain it to him." Matthew punched his fist into his hand, and Hannah shuddered.

"Dear, I do think it's best if you stay with Matthew tonight. If it's okay with him," Aunt Laura tried to soothe her.

"What about you?" Hannah's eyes flew open wider. "What about Aunt Laura?" she pleaded with Matthew.

"He never threatened her before. I'm sure she'll be fine," Matthew said calmingly.

"No, he … before, he didn't have a reason to hurt those I love. He just thought I'd go with him. Now he knows that I won't."

Matthew thought for a moment. "Would you feel better if she goes to the bed and breakfast tonight?"

Her aunt nodded. "I don't mind, dear." Laura patted her niece's hand. "I am not afraid of this Bret, but if it will make you feel better." She leaned in. "I have pepper spray. Got it through security on the plane!"

Hannah laughed nervously and felt somewhat better. She agreed to send her aunt to stay at the nearby B&B. A taxi would take her to Hannah's room first, to collect her bags. Her aunt kissed Hannah's cheek.

"I'll go now, dear. The jet lag is kicking in, and I'm afraid I can't eat a thing with all the upset. Oh, I feel so guilty."

Hannah and Matthew assured her there was nothing to feel guilty about. Her aunt agreed to text as soon as she was safely in the B&B, and she even agreed to ask the taxi driver to accompany her to Hannah's room to collect her bags, though she complained that Hannah was being silly.

"He's not going to come after me, dear," she said confidently.

Then she made her niece promise to call her when she was safely at Matthew's house.

"And call me if you feel afraid, even if it is the middle of the night."

Then Laura walked out of the Otter into the cool night air. As soon as her aunt left, Matthew scooted closer to Hannah. "I hope he comes after us. I want to teach him not to harass you. He doesn't look all that tough."

Hannah just shook her head. She stared at the uneaten fish.

"Matthew," she sighed. Then she looked up into his eyes. "He is a vampire."

"What?" Matthew asked. "That has nothing to do with it. I mean, he could have picked up some odd tricks, sure, but can he really fight?"

"No," Hannah folded her hands over his, and leaned closer. "He doesn't dress up like one. He *is* one. I know you don't believe me." Hannah leaned back, studying him.

Matthew's look of confusion turned to one of horror.

"These marks?" Hannah pointed to her neck. "They are bite marks. Not from plastic fangs, though. Real ones. He was trying to turn me. Make me one of … them. I wanted it. Not anymore, though. I swear, not at all."

Matthew's eyes scanned Hannah's face, searching for the joke, or the truth.

"Lily saw him, that's why she freaked. Go ahead and ask her. She knows he's not hu … human." Hannah pushed her phone toward Matthew.

Matthew punched in Lily's name on the phone. He spoke, watching Hannah carefully. "Lily? Is that you … oh hi, Tom. Um, can I speak to … oh sure … yeah, tomorrow's fine. Sleeping, what …?"

Hannah mouthed, "Congratulations on the engagement."

Matthew stared at her with unbelieving eyes. "Oh, hey, Tom? Congratulations, man. Lily just told us tonight. Yeah, it's gorgeous, a real rock."

He closed the phone. "Congratulations?" he asked, stunned.

"Well, it's important news, you know. Happens once in a life, hopefully." Hannah explained. "So anyway, there's no way she's already asleep. See how freaked she is, she can't even answer the phone."

Matthew shook his head. "This proves nothing. So, she's freaked out. So am I. The bloke tracked you down from San Francisco, Hannah. I'm so relieved you weren't alone."

Hannah shuddered. "Me, too." Then she remembered something and held up her wrist.

"See?" She showed Matthew the ring of purple bruises. "See how unnaturally strong he is? That's why

I'm trying to keep him away from you."

Matthew made a pained face as he examined her darkening arm with concern.

"Bastard," he muttered under his breath. "Listen, Hannah. I can see you believe this ... this myth stuff. But I don't. I'm going to show him for the fiend he is. And not the fiend you think. A human, destructible, wimpy fiend who will run as soon as someone sees through his act."

Hannah closed her eyes. All she could think of was Matthew getting hurt, and her aunt as well. Unless ... unless ... she went with Bret. Then the vampire would leave Matthew and Laura and everyone else alone. Matthew would be okay. Laura would be safe. She herself would be strong enough to protect them once Bret turned her. She looked at Matthew.

"Let's go," she whispered.

Chapter 18 – The End

They were in bed. Hannah was watching the window. An hour earlier, her aunt had called saying she was safely tucked into the B&B, a charming room, and her jet lag had caught up with her. Hannah smiled to imagine her aunt fast asleep, safe from the eyes of that … thing. Hannah tried to shift her position, but Matthew's sleeping arm was around her like a clamp. She thought of going to Matthew's communal kitchen and getting some water, but she soon gave up the idea. She wouldn't be able to get up without waking him.

Hannah was stuck gazing at the window, willing Bret not to come in. She wondered if he could actually enter Matthew's room. She cursed herself for asking Bret into her home in San Francisco so long ago. What she had done was give him an open invitation to her home, wherever that might be. She had slept in Matthew's room so many times, maybe it would be considered her home, and Bret would be able to enter. She wasn't sure.

Maybe he couldn't enter Matthew's room, though, she considered for the thousandth time, still staring at the window. Technically, she didn't really live there, even though some of her clothes were in the closet …

Hannah shifted again, and Matthew's vicelike clamp tightened around her. She better not move any more, she thought, or she wouldn't be able to breathe.

When Bret's pale face finally appeared at the window, it was not a surprise to Hannah. In fact, she was surprised it had taken this long. It was nearly dawn, but Hannah had not slept at all. She watched, hyperalert, as he easily slid the window open, and with no noise, slunk in. He snorted with amusement when he saw Matthew's arm unconsciously tighten around her.

"As if the boy, the human, could keep you," Bret laughed.

"Get away, you fiend. You are no longer invited into my house." Hannah spoke hopefully. But Bret didn't move.

"How many girls have you killed, anyway?" she asked through gritted teeth. "Do you really think I could love such a heartless fiend?"

Bret's face tightened, but then he flitted nearer. He sat on the bed next to her.

"Oh, Hannah. Those are the rules of the human world. Not mine." His voice—the melody of his voice—was so beautiful. She felt she was far away, in a beautiful garden, kissing the pine-scented night. She had forgotten how magical that was. Hannah shook her head. He was kissing her hand. Then he stopped, seeing the dark bruises encircling her arm.

"Did I do that?" he asked, concerned. Then his eyebrows relaxed and his face softened. "No matter. Soon you'll be strong, like me."

He bent down then, down to her neck. Her pulse jumped to his lips. "Let's finish where we left off," he murmured into her neck. Matthew groaned in his sleep.

"No!" Hannah pushed at Bret. "Not here."

"Come into the closet with me. There." Hannah pointed to the little door by the bed. "That way, Matt won't ever know."

Bret threw up his hands. "Fine. But he's your first victim, you know. You'll be hungry." His last words came out in a growl. He traced her red lips with his finger and found the scar here he had bitten her. Then he moved his finger to his own lips and tasted it. Hannah shuddered.

"I've been looking forward to this for a long time," he said exquisitely. "Don't be afraid," he soothed. "It won't hurt ... don't you remember?"

Hannah let him pry her out of Matthew's grasp. Bret sang in a low lullaby to Matthew, and he did not wake up. Enchanted, Hannah thought, watching Matthew's face fall into a more peaceful expression. Like I was.

Hannah took a last look at Matthew and blew a kiss his way. "May you be forever loved and safe," she whispered.

Bret chuckled, "Oh, how you'll think differently in an hour or so." He laughed and opened the closet door. When they were in the tiny space, which was not a closet, Hannah closed the door. Firmly. It clicked.

Matthew and Hannah had joked about this door, saying it was the perfect place to hide from exams, parents, and ex-boyfriends or girlfriends. If you closed it completely, it locked. The porter had a key once, but it was unclear whether anyone knew which ancient key opened this old door.

It was dark in the narrow space, but there was a window at the top, letting in the soft light of the predawn haze.

"Is this …? Never mind," Bret murmured. He found Hannah's neck with his cool, smooth hands.

"Never mind?" Hannah laughed. "But this is your end. And mine."

Bret hesitated.

"This is an old … actually I don't know what it was. I think it was a storage pantry or something," Hannah babbled, feeling strangely free. The sky lightened. Hannah could make out the silhouette of the vampire before her.

"I'm not afraid," she explained. "The story is over. Do you know how it ends?" Bret shook his head, and she saw the dark movement in the night.

"You turn me. Then we die. Matthew is saved." Hannah pointed to the window above them, letting in light. "It looks like the first and only clear morning in England." Hannah laughed drily.

Bret tried the door with one hand. It didn't open.

"It's an old lock. Think you can break it?" she asked.

Bret scowled as he beat at the door with a fist.

"Heavy, isn't it?" Hannah was strangely flippant.

The sky was getting lighter at an fast rate. In fact, the first glow of sun touched Hannah's skin. She was surprised to feel the hand still around her neck grow warm. Bret let go of her neck and pounded on the door with both fists. He smashed into it with all his force. But it did not open.

He looked around frantically. Hannah knew that he didn't have enough space in this narrow room to run at the door. Pounding from the other side stilled Hannah's heart.

"Hannah? Hannah?" a muffled cry came through the

door.

"Matthew!" Hannah screamed. "Don't open the door!"

"Open the door, or the girl dies!" Bret roared.

"I'll get the—wait! I'll get the porter. Don't touch her!" Matthew screamed through the door. Then there was silence.

Hannah began to laugh hysterically.

"The key! It's too late. They'll never find it in time!" The sun now made her arm pink. She held it up to the light. Smoke. Hannah smelled smoke. The vampire tore his hands through his dark curls. He was crazed now. He moved back and forth. He even tried to climb the tiny space, climb the walls. But he could no longer even look up, look at the sky.

Hannah prepared to die. But, she thought, at least she would die a human. The burning smell was stronger. Bret, when he brushed past her, was hot to the touch. Finally, he roared and pulled his clothes off. He curled into a naked ball on the floor and covered himself with his shirt, his pants. But Hannah lifted them off him and stuffed them high up, high in a crack in the wall.

"You loved me!" he screamed, agonized. "You loved me, and now you leave me to die?"

He covered his eyes with his hands. He was light now, lighter than the morning sky. His skin glowed in response to the sun. It was … beautiful, Hannah thought, deranged.

Then his hands lifted away. His eyes, full of light, full of pain, found Hannah's gaze.

She remembered the bar. The sad boy in the corner. She remembered the piña colada, how she laughed when he tasted it and scowled. She remembered kissing him by the statue, wondering at his face in the moonlight.

"You loved me," he said, but now he was asking, not demanding, and his eyes threatened to break apart into splinters of light.

"Yes," Hannah realized. "Yes, I loved you." She was crying.

His face suddenly softened, his eyes cleared with peace. And then he was gone. Ash took his place.

Hannah was not burned. Her hair was singed; that was all.

Minutes passed. Or was it hours? She stood in the light. And then the door opened with a solid groan.

Matthew, pale, stubble on his cheek and wearing his robe, rushed into the narrow space. A sleepy, confused-looking porter stood behind him. An old, iron key swung in his hand.

"Why they haven't sealed off this room I don't know. You be careful missy," he mumbled to Hannah. Then he tipped his head to her, and shuffled out of the room, slamming the old key onto Matthew's bedside table on the way out.

Matthew's eyes searched the small space. He looked up.

"Where ... where ... I heard him. Did he get out?"

Hannah pointed to the ash on the floor.

"The sun," she said, her voice hoarse. Matthew touched the ends of her singed hair.

"What did he do?" he asked. He searched her hands, her pockets. He saw the clothes stuffed in the wall above her. He found no explanations.

"He burned ... he burned ..." Hannah was crying.

And then she started to laugh.

"Han?" Matthew asked gently.

"I'm alive!" she whispered. "I'm alive!"

Matthew stared at the pile of ash.

Chapter 19 – The Beginning

Later that morning, Hannah, Matthew, and her aunt sat at the B&B around a small table. They had all admitted to being ravenous and blamed it on having missed dinner the night before. Hannah felt her newly cropped hair. Hannah had cut her hair in a straight line with Matthew's scissors as soon as she was released from the closet. Then she had taken a shower and retrieved Bret's clothes from the wall.

"Should we burn these?" she had asked.

"Goodwill," Matthew had replied, fingering the silk. She had nodded, but planned to burn them anyway.

Free, she thought. I'm free of him.

"You're not afraid anymore," Matthew had said, after she had dressed. Her expression was smooth, without tension. She looked at Matthew steadily.

"No," she had agreed. "He's not coming back."

Matthew had dressed in silence. Then a text came from her aunt. "Sleep well? Come here for breakfast."

So they went. Hannah was strangely hungry.

"He's gone," she immediately told her aunt. "It's over." Her aunt studied Hannah's face and then hugged her for a long time.

"What happened?" Laura asked.

"A ... fight," Hannah admitted. "He won't come back."

Now they sat around a pink floral tablecloth, waiting for coffee and full English breakfasts to arrive. Laura watched Hannah's face with some concern, and Matthew stared down at his hands.

"So ... a fight? Are you okay?" Laura asked, alarmed.

Hannah remembered him then, the trapped animal. His hot skin, glowing with white-hot light. His eyes searching hers.

"No," she replied to Laura. "But I will be." She slipped her hand into Matthew's, who stared at it, entwined in his.

A text from Lily arrived. "Sleep well? All okay?"

Hannah called back immediately.

"Lil!"

"Han!"

They spoke at the same time, as three English breakfasts and steaming coffee arrived at the table. Hannah's aunt looked ecstatically at the plate heaped with sausages, beans, toast, and mushrooms.

"I'm so sorry I left, I was freaked ..." Lily began.

"I'm so glad you called. I was worried," Hannah said at the same time.

They paused.

"Listen, Lily, it's over. The guy ... moved on. For good. I'm okay ... we all are."

A long pause. Then Lily's hushed voice: "Oh, thank God. But Hannah ..."

"Mmm?" Hannah asked.

"What was ... you know? I think I'll ask you in person."

They made plans to meet later that night at the Otter for uninterrupted fish and chips. Hannah hung up and sighed. She decided she would tell Lily everything. Whether or not Lily would believe her, she was not sure. She fingered her scars. She was tired of lies.

Matthew surprised her by grabbing her phone. He opened it and punched in a name.

"Lil," he said. "It's me ... listen, this is important. Can you tell me ... exactly what you saw last night?"

He paused for a long time. "Mmmhmmm" he mumbled, listening. Hannah tried to distract herself, tried not to listen. She hoped Matthew wouldn't decide she was completely insane.

"What do you want to do today, dear?" Aunt Laura asked her, digging into her sausage. "It's sunny, I noticed. I saw it through my window."

"Oh yeah, we could walk along the river. Or through some of the colleges." Hannah told her aunt of their plan to meet Lily for fish and chips that night, and her aunt's eyes brightened.

"And we move tomorrow, correct?" Laura asked.

Hannah suddenly felt lighter. "That's right. Tomorrow." She smiled.

She gave silent thanks to whatever twist of fate allowed the unopenable closet to be nearby the night before. What if they had already moved? Hannah shuddered. Then, as she listened to Matthew's voice relate the story of the awful night, Hannah wondered if he would still want to move in with her. Knowing she had dated a monster.

Laura patted Hannah's hand.

"Eat, dear. You look like you could use some hot food," she coaxed.

Hannah stabbed a sausage with her fork. Matthew muttered good-bye and handed Hannah the phone, not meeting her eyes. She searched his profile. He was staring at the breakfast before him, his eyes narrowed in concentration. She lamely pushed her fork into the beans.

"Eat, both of you!" Laura pushed the plates toward Matthew and Hannah. "You'll both become skeletons!"

Hannah nibbled at the sausage. Just a few hours ago, she had been convinced she would die.

Matthew looked up then, directly into Hannah's eyes. His expression appeared bewildered. Hannah offered him some coffee, but he shook his head no. She felt her cheeks flush, and she drank her coffee nervously. Her aunt patted her hand.

"See, a little sausage and beans, and the color is back in your cheeks!" she pinched Hannah's cheeks. Then she looked surprised. "When did you cut your hair, dear? I can't believe I didn't notice right away! Must be the jet lag. I like it. It's a serious cut, but it suits you."

"Oh, I just ... did it this morning," Hannah explained. "You know, I couldn't sleep. But ... it's kind of severe."

"I like it," Matthew said, reaching up to finger the chopped ends.

"Really?" Hannah suddenly felt ecstatic—he had talked to her! "Because it's only temporary. I can go to the salon, get it feathered a bit."

"You're worried about that? After all that has happened?" Matthew began to laugh.

"Well, I know you like my hair long." Hannah smiled.

It sounded silly to her, too.

"Oh Hannah, to have you free of that … that thing … that's all I want," Matthew explained.

Hannah smiled, and her aunt pointed at the fried toast. "That thing is loaded with calories," her aunt grinned, "and the most delicious thing on the plate!" Hannah bit into hers, feeling hot butter rush into her mouth. She suddenly felt hungry. As Matthew and Hannah fell to eating, they discussed what to do after breakfast. They decided first to take a walk by the river. Hannah wanted to stay in the sun. No one protested.

"Great idea!" her aunt said enthusiastically.

They got up from the table, and Aunt Laura asked them to come with her to the room.

"It's just so charming, you have to see it!" she gushed, and they walked up the tiny stairs. Matthew reached for Hannah's hand as they entered the decorated room, and Hannah felt grateful as his hand slipped into hers.

"I love it!" her aunt beamed and pointed to the rose-printed wallpaper. "It's so cute and cozy. I'll sleep here tonight, too."

Aunt Laura excused herself to go to the bathroom. Hannah looked up at Matthew.

"So, are you … okay now? I mean, do you understand … everything? Well, do you still want to move in together?" Hannah asked nervously.

"Of course I want to," Matthew said softly. "Even though I'm not sure I understand everything."

Hannah looked down at their hands, which were clasped together.

"I'm so glad you still want to live with me," she said. Matthew kissed the top of her head. When Aunt Laura returned to the room, Matthew announced that he had an idea. He led them downstairs to the reception desk. He asked for a second room, a double room, for the night.

"I think she needs a fresh start," he explained to Laura, "if it's okay with you."

He turned to Hannah. "We don't have to go back to my room, or yours. That is all over now. And tomorrow we'll be in the new place." Hannah nodded. She looked at the tiny reception area, with the wildflowers on the desk, the pictures of flowers on the walls.

"It's perfect," Hannah murmured, "for a new start."

Matthew leaned into Hannah's ear and fingered her hair. "For what it's worth …"

Hannah's green eyes met his.

"I believe you." He paled as he spoke. Hannah grabbed his hand.

"Listen," she said pleadingly. "It doesn't matter anymore. It's … he's … gone."

Matthew nodded. "But just so you know. Lily does, too. We both believe you. And that is important."

He smiled again. The three of them turned to the door. Hannah looked at the sun playing on the doorstep. With Matthew's hand in one hand and her aunt's hand in the other, she stepped into the sun.